# pierced

## sugar and spice ink

## BY EVAN GRACE

# pierced
### sugar and spice ink

BY
EVAN GRACE

# dedication

To my bad boy

# definition of
## PIERCED

*(of the ears, nose, or other part of the body) having had a hole made so as to wear jewelry.*

# one

## GRETA

I turn on my ring light, lay out all my makeup, and quickly prep my face. Once that's all done and dry, I grab the little remote, turning my camera on.

"Hey everyone, I'm so excited to share this new vegan makeup line I just discovered. Naturally Yours is based out of San Diego and gives you a light natural glow."

As I go through the process of putting on the different products, I make sure to describe each one. Once I finish, I set my brush down.

"Don't you just love this? It gives you that, 'is she really wearing makeup,' look. The information and sales links are in my bio. We'll catch you next time."

I turn off the video and quickly watch it and make sure it looks good. Once I upload it, I shut everything off. On my dresser I grab my gray headband and quickly slip it over my brown hair, that is up in a topknot.

My phone pings, signaling a text that just came in, and I grab my phone. It's Sia, the CEO of Naturally Yours. They've invited me to go to Coachella. I'm so excited, I've never been, and I'm looking forward to experiencing it first-hand.

**Sia:** Hey doll, just caught your video and that look is gorgeous on you. I've emailed you your flight information. We'll have a driver at the airport and if you run into any problems, just let us know. We can't wait to see you.

I'm so excited for this.

**Greta:** Sounds great. I can't wait to see you too and thank you again for inviting me.

After tossing my phone on my bed, I look in my closet for something to wear to work. I thumb through my dresses and decide on a cute short peasant dress. I'll pair it with my tan espadrilles that lace up my calves.

Once I'm dressed, I head out into the living room. I pick up my purse, my keys, and head out. Traffic is heavy, so it takes me almost an hour to get to the studio. As soon as I reach it, I park next to Mona's Range Rover.

Inside, the familiar buzz of the tattoo machines can be heard over Hole, playing through the speakers. I spot Mona, bent over a client's arm. Sierra is working on a piece and Heidi is behind the desk.

"Hey, sorry I'm late. Traffic was a nightmare." I lean down, kissing her cheek. "How are things? I've hardly seen you. How's Colton?"

I wasn't super thrilled when Heidi's high school boyfriend showed back up. Especially since he broke my sister's heart when he just up and left their senior year of high school. I'm not gonna lie, if he hurts her again, I will castrate him. He's a huge guy, but for my sister, I'd whoop his ass.

"He's good, and we've just been getting to know each other again." She looks me up and down. "You look so good. I hate you."

I know she's only kidding. Genetics are amazing because Mona, Sierra, and Heidi are all blonde hair, blue eyes, and petite curvy. Miles and me, we're both tall, lean, brown hair, and brown eyes. It makes no sense, but it is what it is.

"Oh, shut up, you're gorgeous and I love the all-over pink," I say, fingering a cotton candy-colored lock of her hair.

In the office, I deposit my purse in the bottom desk drawer and quickly look through pictures to see if any need to be uploaded onto the website. Once that's done, I quickly pop on my brother's social media and share some teasers for his upcoming Detective Jameson novel.

After that, I grab a bottle of water and head out front.

The plane comes to a stop. I gather my things and grab my small suitcase from the overhead compartment. Butterflies begin to take flight in my belly as I step into the aisle, making my way toward the front of the plane.

I get looks when I walk through the airport, but I'm used to it. My body is seventy percent covered in tattoos and it is certainly my canvas. I also have piercings; I have my septum pierced, my dimples, and my ears. Of course, there are the ones that you can't see, which are my nipples, belly button, and clitoral hood.

I'm confident enough to own it and embrace that I'm different—a little boho chic mixed with Kat Von D. My outfit is super adorable, I'm wearing a royal blue, with tiny rainbows all over it, smock waist romper with spaghetti straps. On my feet are a pair of black Converse.

As soon as I reach baggage claim, I spot a driver holding a sign with my name on it. "Hi, I'm Greta."

"Welcome to Palm Springs," he says while tipping his hat, making me smile. "Here, I'll take your suitcase." He grabs it before leading me out into the hot Palm Springs air. He takes me toward a black Escalade and opens the back door for me.

I lean forward, adjusting the vent, and blowing the cool air on me. Most of the clothes I brought, believe it or not, are skimpier than this. I knew it would be hot and crowded, so minimal clothing would be necessary.

He climbs in and then we're off.

I shoot my sisters and brother a text letting them know that I arrived safely. As I watch the passing scenery, I stick my phone back into my purse. A short drive later he pulls into the winding drive of the Palm Hotel & Spa.

Sia waves as we pull up in front of the doors. She's with two other women from her company, but I don't remember their names. My driver opens my door for me and he refuses the tip I try to give him.

He's gone as soon as he sets my suitcase by me. "Enjoy Palm Springs, miss."

"Greta, we're so glad you're here." She pulls me into a hug. "Come meet the other half of Naturally Yours. This is Tiffanie and her wife Mia."

I smile and we exchange greetings and cheek kisses. "It is so nice to meet you. This place is gorgeous."

We head inside and through the lobby. "How was your flight?" Tiffanie asks as they lead me out the back and to what looks like bungalows.

"It was great. Especially with no layovers. How long have you guys been here?" I ask as they open the door and we step inside.

Mia smiles at me. "We got here about three hours ago."

I follow behind her into the gorgeous living room.

"As you can see, we got a place big enough for all of us to stay." They give me the tour and then show me my room. It is bigger than my room in the apartment I share with Heidi.

"This is amazing. What's on the agenda?" I ask as I set my suitcase on my bed and start unpacking, hanging up my outfits. The butterfly wings I brought, per Iris's request, have held up nicely.

"OMG! Those are the cutest things I've ever seen," Sia says as she steps into the bedroom and picks them up. "For our agenda, tonight we're going to go have dinner and then tomorrow the festivities begin.

We got some invites to some of the most exclusive parties. Better rest up."

They leave me to unpack and to take a quick little siesta.

I sip my iced coffee while sitting by the pool. Last night we had a great time. We went to this little Mexican restaurant, and I ate my weight in carne asada tacos and we drank blood orange margaritas.

We had ordered another round when *he* walked in, Jett Hamilton, bad boy action star. I turned away because I certainly didn't want him to see me staring. It was no surprise that he was followed by an entourage of beautiful women.

Of course, I wasn't the only one staring, but the man was gorgeous.

While we finished our drinks, the girls showed me some of the new palates that they'll be releasing.

"These are gorgeous colors." The cheek colors were a soft rose, a shimmery pink, and a light peach.

"We're so excited to launch it. You were the inspiration for the shimmery pink. It's called Greta," Sia told me with a huge smile on her face.

My eyes immediately filled with tears, but I didn't want to ruin my makeup, so I blinked rapidly. "That is the sweetest, most generous thing that anyone has ever done."

"You've been one of our biggest supporters and we're just happy to have you spreading the word about our line," Tiffanie said and held out her glass to clink with mine and then Sia and Mia.

They paid our check, and then we made our way toward the exit. We were almost to the door when I felt eyes on me. I turned to find none other than Jett Hamilton staring at me. Butterflies began to take flight in my belly.

"Come on, Greta." Sia grabbed my hand and dragged me out of the restaurant. We came back to the hotel, where I promptly passed out.

Now I enjoy the quiet of the morning. Since I'm the one who usually closes the store these days, I tend to sleep in till at least ten or eleven.

My phone pings and I pick it up, smiling.

> **Miles:** How's Cali?

I start typing out a response.

> **Greta:** Sunny… Hot. Tell your girl, thank you again for letting me borrow her suitcase.

> **Miles:** She says you're welcome, and anytime. Send us lots of pictures. Love you squirt.

I shake my head. Heidi is my best friend, but my brother and I have always shared a special bond. Maybe it's because we were born so close together. After I send him a smiley face, I head back to our bungalow and get ready for the pool party we're going to.

Let the party begin.

# two

## JETT

I toss the synopsis I just finished reading onto the table in front of me. "I want this role, Josiah."

He's been my manager for the past five years.

"This role would prove to my critics that I *am* a damn good actor."

He sits down across from me with his cup of coffee. "I know. That is why I'm going to get you that script. They're saying whoever gets this role, that their career is going to skyrocket." Josiah takes a sip of his coffee. "There's just one problem. They say you're a risk because of your reputation."

"Bro, that is such shit. What the fuck do they want from me?"

I know I have gotten in trouble before, but usually alcohol was a contributing factor. People fuck with me, and I don't like it.

"Not to be seen around LA with girls who look young enough to be your kids."

They're young, but at least they're twenty-one and that's what I tell him. "They don't want commitment and neither do I."

He sighs in frustration. "Let me think about a way we can tweak your image."

"Yeah, mate. I'm going for a swim." I head outside to the pool at the house I rented for the weekend. We had a party back here last night, but I hired someone to come clean up early this morning so you wouldn't know that a party ever happened.

I dive into the water and begin gliding through it as I swim back and forth. It's been ten years since I've been in America. I came first to do modeling, which I did for three years. Then I got my first acting role, and a passion was born.

My looks had a lot to do with getting me my first break, but I took acting classes, weapons training, and even several forms of martial arts. I've worked on my craft and feel like I'm ready to take my career to the next level.

I'm aware that I have a reputation. I've gotten into "scuffles" with paparazzi before. I got arrested for getting into a fight at a Foo Fighters concert, and then I got a DUI. Then there are the women, I love them, and they love me. I'm an equal opportunity "dater" and every time I go out, it's with a different gorgeous lady on my arm.

Most of them are models or actresses, and all beautiful. They tend to only want what they think they can get from me, which is orgasms—lots and lots of orgasms, and then they go on their way, but not before they sign a nondisclosure agreement.

At first, I wasn't comfortable with it, but the last thing I need is someone talking. It happened right after I made it big with my modeling. First, she accused me of giving her an STD and then that she was pregnant. It was a long painful process, but I finally cleared my name. Now I'm so used to asking the women to sign it that it's no longer a big deal.

I finish my laps and pull myself out of the pool. There's a fluffy white towel waiting on the chair for me, and I use it to dry off. I run my fingers through my wet hair, slicking my hair back.

Back inside, Josiah hands me a protein shake. I chug it down and then set the empty glass on the counter.

"What's the plan today?" I grab a banana off the counter, peeling it open.

"We have a dinner meeting tonight and then tomorrow the parties begin."

I leave him to go shower and get ready for our dinner meeting.

I walk into Los Amigos with Josiah and a bunch of people who happened to follow us inside. The ladies are hot and I wouldn't mind any of them to warm my bed. I reach the table where director, Jonathon Walters, is waiting.

He directed the movie, Summer Heat, that I just finished shooting. This is my chance to talk to him and make the connections to hopefully get me a role I want. I'll do a little schmoozing and hopefully earn myself an audition.

The man stands, followed by the two men that worked on the project. "Jett, good to see you. You remember Cal and Gage." I shake hands with each man and then Josiah follows suit.

"Of course. How are you?"

Once we take our seats and security gets the people that followed us in, to go sit somewhere else so we can talk. Hopefully, the girls will hang around, and maybe they'll want to have a little nightcap at the hotel.

Jonathon orders us a round of drinks and then we start to talk. "Thanks for coming in last week and doing the ADR." That is when you go in and redo dialogue that might not be audible.

"No problem, mate. It was a great film to be a part of."

This was my first step into comedy/action. It's only a supporting role, but it's a stellar cast and should be a box office hit. I play one of the hitmen going after Lisette Coleman. She's gorgeous, and good at what she does, but has the personality of a sloth—she's fucking boring.

"The parties this weekend are going to be sick," Jonathon leans in and says. "Tomorrow I got us an invite to the Corona-sponsored pool party at Zion Estate."

They deliver our drinks and then take our food order. I turn to see if the girls who followed us in are still around, but my eyes land on one of the most beautiful women I've ever seen.

She's built like a model and her arms are covered in ink. Her brown hair hangs down her back with soft waves. She and the women she's with walk toward the front door. Suddenly she stops and turns, allowing me to get a good look at her.

It feels like all the blood in my body heads straight for my cock. My stomach does this weird little flip, and I don't miss the pink tinge of her cheeks, but I'm disappointed when one of her friends grabs her hand, dragging her out of the restaurant.

Josiah leans in. "Do you want me to see what I can find on her?"

Not only is he my manager, but he's also my wingman.

"Yeah, bro."

The brunette stays on my mind the rest of the night, but I know in the morning Josiah will know everything about her.

I climb out of the shower and quickly pat myself dry. With my towel around my waist, I head into my bedroom and slip on a pair of red board shorts. Riffling through my suitcase, I grab my black sleeveless T-shirt.

I'm wearing a hat, so I don't worry about styling my hair. Instead, I just run my hands through my wet hair until it's slicked back. In the kitchen, I find Josiah sitting at the breakfast bar.

"Morning," I say as I grab a coffee cup and pour myself some.

Josiah sits back with a satisfied smile on his face. "I've solved two of your problems. Tell me thank you, Josiah. You're the best manager I've ever had," he says, trying to copy my accent, and of course he does it poorly.

I lean against the counter, laughing. "You're the best manager I've ever had."

He turns his laptop toward me. It's the girl from last night.

"Greta Collins," I say to myself. It looks like she does a lot of makeup and hair tutorials. "Tell me about her."

"She's an influencer. She does piercings at the tattoo studio she runs with her three sisters. She's twenty-six and has never been married and is single. One of her sister's partner is a big-time restauranter in Atlanta. The other's is a stockbroker, and super successful. There isn't so much as a parking ticket." He turns the laptop toward himself again and starts typing. "She's done some modeling."

I look at the pictures, she's a cross between a Victoria's Secret Angel and bohemian princess, who just happens to be pierced and tattooed.

"Her brother, Miles Collins, is a best-selling crime fiction author, I've read his books and they'd translate fantastically on film. All in all, she's from a good, close family."

I nod. "Okay, what else?"

"I have the perfect plan to improve your image." He points to the picture of Greta. "Her. She's going to be at the pool party today. I'll arrange a meeting and if you can tolerate spending some time with her. You bring her when you charter the yacht in Croatia and when you head to Greece for a little R&R before your cologne ad. We'll make sure you're seen together everywhere. Get cozy and make it look and feel real."

I take a sip of my coffee. "You want me to spend time with this girl, make it look real, and that will get me an audition?"

Josiah smiles. "Exactly. Because it'll show you're moving away from that bad boy that everyone thinks you are. Sell that you're falling for this girl and soon you'll be the new 'it' couple. I think she'll be relatable and she's gorgeous. The paps will love her."

I'm not sure I'm down for that, but this role could be a career changer. I'd begin to be taken seriously.

Although, I am looking forward to meeting the tattooed beauty.

# three

## GRETA

With a snap, I shut my blush case and set it on the counter. I lean forward and give myself a once-over. I gave my lids a frosty white look with a light blue liner—it is so retro. My cheeks look sun kissed and my lips are covered in a clear pinkish gloss.

We're heading to a pool party, and I decided to wear the most adorable blue bikini, covered with a white knit cover-up that hits right below my ass. My sandals are gladiators that go up to the top of my calves.

I place some perfume on my wrists, behind my knees, and behind my ears. In the living room, I find Mia and Tiffanie snuggling on the sofa. They're in matching jumpers and high-heeled sandals.

"You guys look great."

They smile and stand up. "So do you," Mia says. "It's not fair. Even in heels, I'm nowhere near as tall as you."

"Trust me, sometimes it is a curse. I don't always get to wear cute heels because most guys don't like it if you show up for a date and you're taller than them."

Sia comes out in a long pink gauzy maxi dress. We all pose for pictures and then head out to a huge golf cart that is waiting for us. I climb on the back, slip my sunglasses on, and hold on as the driver takes off.

A half mile away, we begin to slow down. I look toward the front and that is when I see cars and golf carts lined up ahead of us. "Did I mention there's a red carpet and photographers?" Sia leans in and says.

"Oh my god. Now I am nervous," I say as my leg starts to bounce.

She grabs my hand. "Don't be nervous. We're just going to a party."

Of course I know it is so much more than that. This is a chance to network a bit, gain new followers, and possibly make connections.

While we wait, a pair of waiters pull up next to us and hand us glasses of champagne. Of course, we have to take a selfie. It takes ten minutes before it's our turn. Sure enough, there are some photographers and instead of a red carpet, it's hot pink.

The four of us climb off and then we walk the carpet. I pose and smile and couldn't tell you what happened because I swear I blacked out a little bit. Next thing I know is the girls lead me toward our private cabana.

Mia pops the cork on the champagne, and she pours us each a glass. She holds her glass up and we all follow suit.

"To an amazing weekend."

We clink glasses and then I swallow the crisp cold drink down.

It's a few hours later when I feel eyes on me. I'm standing at the bar getting a drink. I want to look around, but I'm not sure if I want the attention from whoever is looking at me.

I order a frozen lemonade and vodka and once he hands it to me, I turn around, slamming into a hard body. Two strong arms wrap around me, stopping me from falling backward.

"Whoa... I've got you."

I look up into the face of none other than Jett Hamilton.

"You okay?"

Oh god, I think my vagina just started singing. "Ahem... I'm good, thanks." My cheeks feel like they're on fire right now. He rights us and I step back. "Thanks again for saving me."

I start to walk away, but he grabs my hand and I try to ignore the tingling feeling I get from his hand in mine.

"Tell me your name. Mine is Jett." He brings my hand to his mouth, kissing the back of it.

"I know who you are, Jett, and I-I'm Greta." I pull my hand back from his grasp. "It was nice meeting you."

He watches me as I walk around him, and back to the girls.

A giant white blowup swan sits in the pool by our cabana. "Sia, can I use this?"

"Yeah, they just brought them out for whoever wants to get in the pool." She smiles before turning back to the man she's talking to.

After removing my sandals, I slip off my cover-up and pad my way to the pool. There are no stairs so I walk right into the water. I hop onto the swan, put my sunglasses on, and close my eyes to soak in the sun.

The sun has set and there are twinkle lights and torches everywhere. I'm exhausted, but the girls are still partying it up. I don't want to be rude by leaving, so I curl up on a little bed in the cabana, listening to the music and people-watching.

I type a quick text to Heidi.

**Greta:** Hey girlie, I hope things are going well. I miss you and do I have a story for you.

"Are we that boring that you're falling asleep?" I recognize that sexy voice from earlier.

I push myself up to sitting, feeling slightly embarrassed. "I—uh... no, I'm just not a big drinker and between the drinks and the sun, I'm just a little sleepy."

Jett walks farther into the cabana. "Can I sit?"

My heart beats wildly in my chest. "Sure." I scooch over so he can join me. "Are you having fun?" I ask lamely. Oh god, he's going to walk away because I'm such a nerd.

"It's been alright, but it would've been better if a certain brunette didn't hide from me all day." His cerulean blue eyes sparkle under the glow of the twinkle lights. Jett reaches out, fingering a loose strand of my hair. "I love your ink."

"Thanks. Some people think it's excessive, but I love it. My sisters are the ones that have done all of them, and each one means something to me."

He signals to one of the waitstaff. "Can we get a couple of waters, bro?"

God, I love his accent.

Jett turns back to me. "Your sisters are tattoo artists?"

I smile and nod. "Yep, as far as I'm concerned, they're the best in the south."

"Do you do tattoos?" The waiter brings us our water and he thanks him. He hands me mine.

I shake my head. "No, I'm not artistic at all. I do the piercings and help man the front desk."

Jett grabs my hand and turns it side to side, looking at the design. It's a bouquet of each of my siblings' birthday month flower, and mine.

"My oldest sister, Mona, did that one."

"It's beautiful." His thumb rubs back and forth across my wrist. Can he feel my pulse pounding? "Is this your first time at Coachella?"

I'm going to have an orgasm just from the way he says... well, who am I kidding, from the way he says anything—I mean my god, his voice.

"It is. I'm really excited."

"I want to meet up with you tomorrow. Are you cool with that? There's also a party tomorrow, I want you to be my plus one. What do you think?"

His eyes go to my lips when I nervously lick them.

"Jett," two feminine voices whine. "We've been looking for you all night."

Right in front of me, the one climbs on his lap, and the other sits next to him. I grab my bag and stand up. "I think I'll pass." With fake bravado I didn't know I possessed, I walk out of the cabana, go find the girls, and tell them I'm not feeling well.

Sia offers to come back with me, but I know she really wants to stay.

"No, stay. I'll be fine." She doesn't look like she believes me, but I gave her a dazzling fake smile. "Have fun. I promise I'll be fine. I just want to rest up before tomorrow."

I head out front, and there is a golf cart waiting to drive me back to the hotel. He's just turning around when the cart jostles and I find Jett climbing on next to me.

"Umm... what are you doing?" I look around for the girls, but don't see them.

He rests his arm on the back of my seat. "We were interrupted, I wasn't done talking to you yet."

I turn in the seat to look at him, my god he's beautiful. "Does that happen a lot. Women 'interrupting' you?" I'm aware I am being a brat. I don't know where it came from. "Sorry, that was rude." Oh great, and now I've probably scared off the hot movie star.

Jett grabs my chin and turns me to face him. "You weren't rude. It happens sometimes. People convince themselves they have free access to me. I won't lie, I've enjoyed it and have welcomed it, but that doesn't mean people can get in my space whenever they want."

The golf cart comes to a stop. "This is me."

He climbs off and holds his hand out to me.

Like a gentleman, he helps me down, and then leans down, kissing my cheek. "I will see you tomorrow and don't worry, I will find you."

All the way back to the bungalow, I swear my feet don't touch the ground, I fucking float.

# four

## JETT

I hop off the treadmill and use the towel hanging over it to wipe the sweat from my face. Last night when those girls interrupted my talking with Greta I'd about lost it on them.

Normally, I would not care, but every second I spent with her I knew I was going to agree to Josiah's plan. She was sweet, but a little sassy and I just knew she was going to be a lot of fun.

In the kitchen I find him sitting at the counter. "I'll do it."

He sets his phone down. "Do what?"

"Fake a relationship with Greta. I'll talk to her about it tonight." I pour a cup of coffee.

"Absolutely not. You can't tell her." Josiah stands up and comes around the counter. "You're an actor, you can sell it, but I think to keep it looking authentic she can't know." He picks up his phone. "Give me a day or two to get the wheels in motion. I know you hate the paparazzi, but they need to see you two together and get the pictures to sell this."

I turn to head to my bedroom to shower, but Josiah stops me. "This means you have to keep it in your pants. No one but her."

I've never made promises to anyone. I don't date so I never have to commit, but I could get behind learning what makes Greta come and come, and all the ways I can make her do it. "I can do that."

I smile as I head back to my room. I'm going to enjoy this.

It's a while later when I step out of my room dressed in a pair of blue-gray chino shorts and a white short-sleeve button up shirt. I throw on my black Nike snapback and slip on my black Chuck Taylors.

I'm dying to know what Greta will be wearing. Hopefully something that shows off her sexy body. Yesterday, when she'd been in just her bikini, I'd gotten an instant hard-on. That's why I had avoided her most of the day. My body couldn't behave itself. Of course, she thinks I thought she was avoiding me.

I hear several voices and know some of my mates have shown up. The minute I open my door, I can smell the pungent scent of weed. I don't partake often, but today I will.

"What's up, fellas," I say as I step into the living room.

I take the offered joint, and then we begin to party.

There are beautiful women everywhere, but I'm on the lookout for a tattooed, brunette beauty. Josiah got Sia, the women that came with Greta's number. She promised him she'd text where they'd be.

All I know is that between the weed, the sun, and the beer I've drank, I am feeling good. Now I just need to find the girl. This is the only place celebrities can come and we're not hounded by fans.

We walk through the crowd and head to the VIP section. I know for sure that is where I'll find Greta. I've started following her on Instagram and she's a natural. She has this aura around her that just captivates you.

Fuck, I've had too many brews, that's my problem and I need to get thoughts of her aura out of my head. We weave through the crowd and I keep a look out for her.

Once we're in VIP, I find her immediately. She definitely stands out in a crowd and when she sees me her face lights up and she waves at me. I stride over to her and take her in. She's dressed in a light blue jumper that ties at her shoulder with a bikini top underneath.

She's got on a pair of Air Force 1's with blue butterflies all over them. Her hair hangs over her shoulder in a thick braid, and she's got a fedora on her head.

"Hey beautiful." I lean in and kiss her lightly on the lips, holding it to let others see. Of course, I ignore the way my heart begins to hammer in my chest at the taste of her on my lips.

I pull away and reach out, using my thumb to wipe off the lip gloss that got smeared above her lip.

"H-Hi," she stutters out.

"Sorry, your lips just looked too kissable. How are you?" I wrap my arm around her waist. "Is this okay?" I should've asked her before, but I already like touching her too much.

Greta nods. "Did you just get here?" she asks as I lead her toward my friends, who are now talking to hers—this is perfect.

"About two hours ago. My mate." I point to Bruno Nixon. He's an actor I met my first year here and lived together at one time. "He rented a RV so we were hanging out there."

"We came by golf cart. This has been the craziest experience ever." She smiles and shakes her head.

"Why do you say that?"

Greta shrugs. "I've never been to parties where there are famous people everywhere. The bungalow we're staying in is bigger than my apartment. This morning we went to something called a gift lounge and got a bunch of free stuff—nice stuff. I guess I'm just a little overwhelmed by it all."

Sia comes up to us. "Can I take a picture? You two look so cute together."

I nod, and she holds up her phone.

"Smile."

We do and she takes a couple of photos of us. She texts them to Greta and she holds her phone up to show me.

Fuck, we look pretty fucking good together. Yes, this is going to work nicely—unless of course this is all an act, but I highly doubt it. I lead us off to the side, but don't let go of her. "You said you were overwhelmed?"

Greta nods.

"Well you look like you fit right in."

"Not at all." She shakes her head. "I honestly probably looked like a kid in a candy store. Most of the stuff I got is actually for my sisters, brother, and niece and nephew."

Why do I like that she thought about her family and not herself? In Hollywood, you meet a lot of people who only care about what they can get. I've been used by people who said they were friends and I've done the same, of course that was when I was first starting out. I'm not proud of it, and regret it, but it taught me about the man I didn't want to be.

"Come get a drink with me." I don't bother asking, I just lace my fingers with hers and we walk up to her friends. "We're heading to the beer garden by the stage."

"I'll catch up with you guys," Greta says as we start walking away.

The one who took our picture calls out. "Have fun, we'll meet up soon."

We weave through the crowd; I keep her close because people are taking our picture and videoing us. This is one of the downsides to what I do, but for Josiah's plan to work this is perfect. Once we reach the beer garden, I order us a couple of beers and then we take them to a table in the corner—it's all outside so we're not really hidden, but hopefully she feels a little comfortable.

"To new friends." I hold up my beer to her and we clink them together.

Greta smiles at me as she brings the bottle to her lips. I watch her throat work as she swallows some down. There are only two days for me to get her to commit to hang out with me.

I give her my signature smile—the one that has helped me get lots of pussy over the years and lean toward her. "You are so fucking beautiful."

She shakes her head and leans toward me. "Are you flirting with me, Mr. Hamilton?"

I throw my head back, laughing because she is saucy… I like it. "Maybe I am. Would it be so bad?"

"No, at least I don't think so." Greta winks at me before taking a drink of her beer.

I grab her hand that's on the table. "I have to ask, since you're a piercer, have you ever pierced someone's cock?"

Greta rolls her eyes at me. "Oh my god. You're such a guy. Yes, I've done Apadravya, the perineum, and… the Prince Albert." She drags out and then looks down at my crotch area. "I'll pierce you if you want."

I immediately cover myself. "Oh no, no needles will be coming near my cock and balls." She's funny and I like it. I rake my eyes over the piercings that she has that I can see; her septum, her dimples, and of course her ears—I've never been a big fan of them, but hers are soft and feminine—a thought occurs to me. "Tell me, do you have any piercings I can't see?"

Her cheeks turn the most adorable shade of pink. She shakes her head. "You'll have to earn that knowledge." Greta brings her bottle to her lips, but I don't miss the grin.

The rest of our group joins us, breaking the connection between us. The women grab her hand, pulling her away from me. We all head back over to VIP and they drag Greta over to the fence so they can watch whoever it is on stage.

I'm ready to join them, but I spot Josiah. Of course, he's the only person at Coachella in suit pants and dress shirt. We share a bro hug and then he signals to go stand off to the side.

"You're not really dressed for a festival," I tell him.

He shakes his head. "I'm on twenty-four-seven. I got to make you that money because when you make money, I make money." He looks toward Greta and then back at me. "Well... do you think you want to spend some time with her?"

I turn to look for her and find her dancing with the other girls. "Hell yeah." I turn back to him. "Set it up."

The man disappears into the crowd, and I can only shake my head. He's something else, but man, he gets the job done. I make my way toward Greta, looking forward to getting between her legs and seeing exactly where else she's pierced.

# *five*

## GRETA

Sia and I sing along to Greta Van Fleet—sweat rolls down my back and down my butt crack, but I don't care because this has been such a fun day. I've danced and sang so much I'm sure my voice will be hoarse tomorrow.

Jett has always been close. Earlier, he grabbed my hand and drug me to the food trucks to grab something to eat. We ate shrimp tacos with a siracha sauce that was so good.

The more time I spent with him, the more comfortable I got. I'm tall for a woman, but next to him I feel small. He's at least six foot three and built like Alan Ritchson. His light brown hair that's a little past due for a haircut, peeks out of his black hat.

While we ate, he had his sunglasses off, and I was mesmerized by his blue eyes that switched from a cerulean blue to turquoise—depending on the way the sun was shining on his face.

I bought my sisters, Victoria, Lainey, and Iris these beautiful bracelets. I bought little Maximum a T-shirt from one of the tents. Jett took care of me all afternoon, making sure I had water, and kept me blocked the best he could when people took pictures or videos of us.

Jett apologized over and over, and that he was used to it and knew I wasn't, which I assured him it was okay, and I appreciated him looking out for me. Although it did kind of freak me out that people were doing that.

Now we're back in VIP and the band playing is my sister, Sierra's, favorite. I've always been more of an everything kind of girl, except country... sorry not sorry. It is just not my thing.

I turn to look for Jett and see that there is a man in a suit talking to him. The guy walks away and then he comes back to me. Did he practice that swagger until he nailed it?

I let out a surprised yelp as he wraps his arm around my waist and pulls me so my back comes in contact with his chest.

"Hey babe," he says with his lips lightly touching my ear. "These guys are great. They sound like Zeppelin."

Turning in his arms, I smile up at him. "They do. Sierra is obsessed with them."

I dance to the music, the whole time with my back plastered to his front. Jett moves with me, but I wouldn't say it's dancing—it is more of a sway, but I like it.

Once the band leaves the stage, he leans in. "Do you want to go walk around?"

"Yeah, let me just check with the girls."

He lets me go and I immediately miss the feel of his hard chest against my back. What is that? I've never had that sort of reaction to someone before. I wrap my arm around Sia's waist.

"Hey, Jett and I are going to walk around, do you want to come with?"

She looks behind me. "No, you go have fun with the hot movie star. We'll be right here, but if we move, I'll text you."

After she kisses my cheek, I turn and take Jett's offered hand. We walk toward the Ferris wheel. He calls out to a couple ahead of us, and that's when I realize it is Hollywood's *'it'* couple, Director Troy Martin and his leading lady, Jacqueline Monét.

They all share hugs and then he introduces them to me. "This is Greta. She's with Naturally Yours cosmetics."

I try to hide my surprise that he knows that.

They both shake my hand and Jacqueline does a double cheek kiss. "It's nice to meet you both." Can Jett feel me tremble? I'm freaking nervous. She just won an Oscar last year and his movies are phenomenal.

The three of them make small talk, but the whole time, Jett's thumb strokes the top of my hand. Does he even realize he's doing it? They leave us and he smiles at me. "Sorry. It was shop talk."

"That's okay. I wouldn't have known what to say anyway."

Jett turns me so we're facing each other. "Don't be nervous, they're just normal people. You're not nervous around me."

I shrug. "I don't know, I just feel comfortable around you." I'm mortified I just said that, but he surprises me when I look up at him.

His face lights up. And why do I like it, and I mean really like it? "I'm glad." He leans in and kisses my cheek. I feel him inhale, and goose bumps pop up all over my body. "You smell like mango."

"Good, I'd hate to smell like BO or something."

Jett laughs and pulls me into a hug. "You're funny."

He lets go me and I do a little curtsy. "Come on, let's walk around."

That's exactly what we do.

My back hits the wall of the RV as Jett ravishes my mouth. I've never been kissed like this in my life, like if he doesn't kiss me, he'll die. His tongue brushes mine, and I swear I have a mini orgasm.

Earlier, the girls said they were heading back to the hotel. Jett told them that he would get me back there safely. He wanted us to be alone, and his buddies gave us the keys to the RV.

The moment we stepped inside, his lips were on mine, which leads us to now. He grabs me behind each thigh, lifting me easily. His erection is hard between us, and I moan as he presses it against the apex of my thighs.

I should stop this. I don't want to be like the girls who throw themselves at him just because he's a movie star. There is just one problem, I can't seem to stop myself.

Jett's hand palms my breast and my nipples harden. He gives it a pinch through the thin material of the romper I'm wearing. His cock continues to rub against me as he pinches my nipple, discovering my nipple ring, and bites at my lips.

"Oh, fuck yes, babe. I knew you were going to be full of surprises."

He gives the hoop a little tug, making me cry out against his mouth. Jett likes that and gives a little growl as he tugs on it again. His lips travel along my jaw and up to my ear.

"Let's get out of here," he whispers. "We'll go back to my hotel."

In my head, I'm saying no, but my mouth says, "Okay."

He sets me back on my feet and, after we get the RV keys back to his friends, his driver meets us by the gate. Jett keeps hold of my hand and we're both quiet as we head to his hotel.

We reach the Ritz Carlton, and the driver opens the door for us, but Jett grabs my hand and helps me out. The inside of the hotel is gorgeous. As he leads us to the elevators, I don't miss the people watching us as we walk by. He just holds me close, trying to shield me from the ones pointing their cameras at us.

At the elevators, security meets us, and they stand guard as we wait for the doors to open. Jett's arm stays wrapped around me and when the doors finally slide open, he leads me in, and security blocks anyone else from getting on.

Once the doors shut, he wraps me in his embrace and kisses me softly as we ride up to my floor. The doors slide open, and he pulls me off. On quick feet, we hustle toward the door near the end of the hall.

Jett pulls the keycard out and looks at me. "We don't have to do anything. Just know that there are no expectations."

Instead of answering him, I snatch the keycard out of his hand and use it to let us inside his suite. The moment the door shuts, he lifts me into his arms and carries me into the bedroom. He tosses me on the bed and Jett follows me down, covering my body with his.

He settles between my legs as my heart starts to beat rapidly in my chest. Is this really happening? Am I about to have sex with Jett after only knowing him for a day?

This isn't like me, but there is something about him—It has nothing to do with him being an actor, and everything to do with the way he's treated me since we met.

Jett's lips make their way down my neck, and I tip my head to the side to give him better access. He nips at my overheated flesh, making me cry out. I wrap my legs around his hips and rock against his rock-hard cock.

He grabs my wrists and shackles them above my head and presses his hips snugly against me, and suddenly I'm unable to move. My heart starts to race and my pussy spasms. Jett pulls back and looks down at me with an intense look.

"Are you ready to get fucked, baby?" His voice is thick, and his accent is even heavier.

I nod and lick my lips in anticipation.

He shakes his head. "I need the words. I need you to say it."

<h1 style="text-align: center;">Six</h1>

# JETT

I wait for her answer as my dick throbs in my shorts. I'm so hard right now and can't wait to sink inside her pussy. The first time will have to be quick because my balls are aching, and I know I'm going to come as soon as I'm inside her wet heat.

"Y-Yes, I'm ready to get fucked," Greta says before I attack her mouth again. Fuck, I love the way she kisses me—like she's fucking starved for me and can't get enough.

I pull back, unbutton my shirt, and pull it off. A moan slips past my lips when she reaches up and drags her fingernails down my chest. With quick movements, I peel her romper down to her waist, pull off her bikini top and take a moment to take in her beauty.

Greta's got gold hoops in each nipple, a diamond in her belly button, and beautiful ink covering most of her upper body.

I lean down, wrapping my lips around her nipple. Her back arches off the mattress as I suck it deep into my mouth.

With each pull, she grinds harder against me, making the most delicious sounding mewls. I release it with a pop and switch to the other, but this time I grab the gold hoop, tugging it with my teeth.

I reach in between us and slide my hand inside her panties. My fingers slide over another piercing. Pulling back, I smile down at her. "You're full of surprises." I push up on my knees and pull her outfit and panties, down her legs, and toss them to the floor.

She's a vision. Greta is like my very own tattooed Victoria's Secret model. I grab her thighs and push her legs out and back, wasting no time to get my first taste of her pussy.

The second her arousal is on my tongue, I moan against her wet flesh. Her fingers slide through my hair, and she grabs my head, lifting her pussy closer to my mouth.

Greta comes with a sharp cry the moment I push one finger inside her. She rides the wave as I suck her clit into my mouth, sucking hard. When it finally begins to slow, she tries pushing my head away.

"N-No more," she pants.

I kiss my way back up her body and I kiss her lips, letting her taste herself on my lips and tongue. She licks her cum off as she reaches between us and quickly undoes the button of my shorts.

Her hand slips inside and my eyes want to roll back in my head. Greta palms me and slowly moves her hand up and down. Fuck, I want to come, but I want to do it inside her pussy for the first time.

Using willpower I didn't know I had, I hop off the bed and drop my shorts. I grab a condom, quickly open it, and then slide it down my shaft. Crawling back onto the bed, I crawl over her and reach down between us.

I rub my dick through her arousal and then place the head of my cock into her and then begin to slowly work myself in and out of her. Damn, she's fucking tight, hot, and wet.

Grabbing her leg and pulling it up higher, I bottom out inside her. Greta cries out and I silence her with my mouth as I begin to fuck her in smooth, hard thrusts. She feels so good and the desire to come hits me like a ton of bricks.

"Baby, please tell me you're close," I whisper against her lips.

Greta reaches behind me and grabs my ass in both hands. She begins to fuck herself on my cock. I swallow her whimpers as the tingling begins at the base of my spine.

It happens so fast. She begins to ripple around my dick. She gets really wet and then she begins to come. Pulling her mouth from mine, Greta moans long and loud. My own orgasm is triggered, and I come with a shout, thrust into her hard, as my cum fills the condom.

I bury my face in her neck as I try to get control of myself. She wraps her arms and legs around me, hugging me tightly to her body. Normally at this point I'd be casually hinting to them to get up, dressed, and head out.

Of course, that is after having them signed an NDA, which most of the time they sign it before anything happens. It's the most awkward part of the evening. You know, "Hey, let's fuck, but then here, sign this."

"Am I crushing you?" I whisper against her ear.

Greta shakes her head. "Nope, not at all."

I pull back and smile down at her. "Let me get rid of the condom, and I'll be right back. Do you want something to eat or drink?"

"Maybe some water and I could maybe eat something."

Finally, a woman who isn't afraid to say what she wants. I lean down, kissing her one more time before climbing off the bed and walking into the bathroom. After disposing of the condom, I take a piss and then wash my hands.

Back in the bedroom, I find Greta right where I left her, looking delectable in all her naked glory. I crawl back onto the bed and lie down on my side, facing her when she rolls to face me.

"What are you hungry for?" I hold her gaze as I rub my hand slowly up and down her body. Her skin is soft and smooth, I could touch her all night and not get tired of it.

She smiles and shrugs. "I'll honestly eat anything."

"What about a burger and fries?" I ask her and she nods. Grabbing the phone, I order us a couple of burgers, fries, and milkshakes.

Our food arrives a while later and we snuggle together on the love seat, eating burgers and fries together. The best part is looking at her naked tits the whole time.

Because who wouldn't like eating with that view?

I feel Greta stir beside me, and I pull her into my arms, snuggling her close. Last night after we finished our burgers, we made out like a couple of horny teenagers. I fucked her from behind while she was kneeling on the love seat.

She came so hard that she forced my orgasm right out of me. I carried her into the bedroom and tossed her on the bed. We snuggled together under the sheets, chest to chest.

"Which tattoo was your first?" I asked her as I wrapped my arm around her waist, drawing her closer. It was way too intimate, something I've avoided with the other women I've slept with, but I need her to agree to come with me, which means she needs to believe this.

I know, that makes me a fucking prick, but I hope she'll understand why I did it. This part is one that I really want and could open the door for more serious roles—don't get me wrong, I love doing action movies, and they've made me lots of money, but I'm ready to test my acting chops.

Focusing back on Greta, I ask again. "Tell me?"

She held out her arm, pointing to a green four-leaf clover. "My oldest sister Mona did this the day I turned eighteen. After the first one, I guess you could say I became addicted."

I traced it with my fingers. "All your ink is beautiful."

Greta blushed the most beautiful shade of pink. "Thank you. I'm proud of each piece I have."

"What about your piercings? Who did those?"

She snuggled in under my chin. "My mentor, Lexi. She did each one and taught me everything I know."

I kissed her forehead and hugged her close. "When do you head back to Atlanta?"

"Monday night, why?" She ended it with a jaw-cracking yawn.

"What if I told you that I'd like to spend more time with you?" I rubbed my lips against hers. "Is that something you'd be interested in?"

At first, she didn't say anything, just looked at me with wide eyes. I was beginning to think I made a mistake until her lips tipped up into a smile.

"Do you mean like hang out with you here?"

God, she was fucking adorable. "Yes, but what would you say if I told you I want you to join me on a little trip I'm taking?"

Greta nodded. "Okay, where are we going?" she asked while tracing my nipple with her finger.

Wrapping her hair around my finger, I told her. "First, I'm meeting some friends in Croatia and we're chartering a yacht for three days. Then I'm heading to Greece for a little R&R before a photo shoot." I tucked her hair behind her ear. "What do you think?"

"I-I-I don't know what to say. Are you sure you want me tagging along?" She chewed on her bottom lip.

I grabbed her and pulled her on top of me, wrapping my arms around her. "I wouldn't have asked if I didn't really want you to come. Do you have a passport?"

Shit, I didn't think of that. Even if we expedited it, we still wouldn't have it in time.

"You're in luck, because I always carry it when I travel." Greta crossed her arms over my chest and rested her chin on them. "I'd need to talk to my sisters. We all do our part to run the studio and I can't leave them hanging."

I liked that she said that. It shows the kind of person she is. "Absolutely. The jet we're taking doesn't leave until Monday morning."

The smile she gave me lit up her whole face. "I'll call my sisters tomorrow."

I gave her a squeeze and rolled us, so I was in between her legs, and it was a long time before I let her sleep.

Now the sun peeks through the curtains and Greta rolls in my arms so we're chest to chest.

"Good morning," she whispers before kissing my chest.

"Morning." I kiss the top of her head.

Yeah, this is definitely going to work.

# seven

## GRETA

My Lyft pulls up in front of my hotel. Jett wanted to bring me back, but I didn't want the attention. Especially when it would be obvious, I spent the night with him. He attacked my mouth as we said goodbye at his door. We've made plans to meet up later and I pinch myself because last night seems like a dream.

Jett didn't seem like a movie star, or the bad boy that the media makes him out to be. He was sweet, funny, and attentive. I felt so comfortable with him, I agreed to go with him to Croatia... holy shit.

Reaching our bungalow, I let myself in, I'm prepared for the girls to bombard me with questions. Instead, I find them sitting on the patio with breakfast on the table.

"Good morning," they holler in unison.

Sia waves her hand in a "come here" motion. "We ordered you breakfast, come eat."

My stomach growls and I drop my bag by the door. On bare feet I make my way outside, taking a seat across from Mia. "Did you have a good night?"

"I did. What about you guys?" I spoon some eggs on my plate and then grab a blueberry muffin.

Tiffanie hands me the butter. "We left right after you and we ordered pizza and ate it by the pool."

They tell me about the agenda today. We're going to stay here until after lunch and that'll give me a chance to call Mona and then take a nap. We finish eating and I'm thankful they haven't asked questions.

In my room, I grab my phone and lie on my bed. Mona answers right away. "Oh my god. Girl, your picture is everywhere," she shouts. "How the heck did you meet Jett Hamilton?"

"Geez, calm down, weirdo. We met at a party and then ran into each other at the festival. I've enjoyed getting to know him." Shit, how do I tell her that he wants me to go to Croatia with him? I hope they're cool with it because I really want to go.

"Well, take it from me, the guy really likes you. I could tell from the way he kept looking at you in all the pictures we've seen." Mona talks to her man, Joaquin, in the background. "You look great in all the pictures."

I smile as I fall back on the mattress. "He's so different than what the media portrays him as. Every time someone was filming us or taking our pictures, Jett tried to keep me protected. I don't know how he can stand it."

"I'm sure it's something they just get used to. How have the shows been?" We're all huge music fans with an eclectic variety of favorites.

"They've been great. Imagine Dragons was my favorite." Rolling to my side, I prop my head up with my hand. "This whole experience has been crazy. It's not just meeting Jett either. We went to a pool party, where no one swam. The girls took me to this place where we got lots of free goodies. I, of course, got you all something."

"You're so sweet, little sister."

I start chewing on my thumbnail as I summon up the courage to tell her about the trip. It's not like she's my mom, but I respect her opinion so much. "So… I have something I want to talk to you about."

She's quiet for a second. "Sure, is everything okay?"

"It's all good, I promise. How possible would it be for me to take a little more time off? Jett's invited me to go to Croatia with him on a yacht he's chartering, and I really want to go."

Mona doesn't say anything at first, and I begin to freak out.

"Oh wow," she finally says. "Do you feel safe going with him?"

"I do, and I know he has a bit of a reputation, but he's been so sweet to me. I'm not sure a guy like him has to work hard for female attention." I'm also not going to tell her we slept together already, even though it's not like she'd judge me.

"If you want to go, go. We'll cover you. Maybe we could even see about getting a guest piercer in. You've been there for all of us when we've needed you. We never know when you could get a chance like this again. Do you need anything from us?"

God, I love my family. We stick together and take care of each other. "No, I think I have enough clothes. I just may need to find somewhere to do my laundry. We fly to Croatia on Monday, and I think dock the boat then."

"My sister, jet-setting with a movie star. I'm so excited for you. Make sure you take lots of pictures and call us when you get there." She laughs softly. "Gee, I sound like Mom."

"You do, but yes, I'll call when we get there. I'm going to ship all of your gifts to you, so I don't have to worry about it."

We hang up, and then I toss the phone to the side before falling into an exhausted sleep.

I decide to leave my hair down with the sides braided and pinned to the side, giving me an almost faux hawk look. I throw on a pair of hot pink bootie shorts and layer up two crop tank tops, one white and one black. On my feet, I throw on my black Chuck Taylor hi-tops.

I'd be worried about being so skimpily dressed if I didn't see girls and guys dressed in a lot less than me. Once I rub some shimmering lotion all over my body, I head out into the living room. Smiling, I see the girls dressed similarly to me.

Tiffanie holds up her hands. "Photo sesh," she cries.

Mia rolls her eyes while smiling at her wife.

We pose for several pictures, and we all post them to our social media, tagging their company. I smile as I look through them. We are some good-looking women. There's a knock at the door while Sia starts pouring us some champagne.

Mia answers it, and I freeze when Jett and another guy step inside our bungalow. He comes right to me, pulling me into his arms. Right in front of the others, he kisses me deep. My toes curl, and I'm dazed as he pulls away.

"Hi, beautiful," he says quietly.

"Hi." I smile up at him. "What are you doing here?"

"We have a golf cart to take us to the festival grounds and wanted to see if you wanted a ride." He looks at the other girls. "There is room for you all."

Jett introduces his friend, Nate, to us. "He's a fucking brilliant musician." He claps him on the shoulder.

Sia pours them a glass of champagne too, and we drink them down before heading out to the golf cart. Jett takes the seat next to me and wraps his arm around my shoulders while his friend cozies up to Sia.

Then we make our way to the grounds.

# eight

## JETT

Greta sleeps soundly with her head in my lap. We have an eleven-hour flight ahead of us. I should be sleeping along with everyone else, but I can't. My mum has always said I didn't like sleeping much, even as a boy.

The past twenty-four hours have been crazy but a fucking blast. The music was on fire—we danced and sang all night. I can't remember the last time I've had that much fun.

Josiah texted me early this morning to show me some of the pictures and videos that were being posted online. So far, the attention has been positive. Everyone wanted to know who the mystery girl was and if we were serious.

A lot of the pictures were of us touching and kissing, looking like a real couple. It was just what I wanted, but it also gave me a slightly sick feeling, but I ignored it. I wasn't going to hurt her, and when the time was right, I'd tell her everything.

I wanted her to stay with me last night after we all left the festival, but since we were leaving early this afternoon, she wanted to hang out with the girls, which I understood. They're the ones who flew Greta out here. It was probably a good thing because I got a good night's sleep, and I knew that once Greta and I were together, I was going to want to be inside her every chance I got.

This morning Josiah gave me the itinerary for my trip. Damn, I'd be lost without him. He's always watched out for me, and he has got this trip planned completely, so I don't have to do anything but show up. The man also got Greta and me the best accommodations. I can't wait to surprise her with it.

One nice thing about being a celebrity is people go above and beyond to get you what you need and get you into the most beautiful places. Hell, I grew up in a beautiful suburb of Auckland, New Zealand.

I focus back on the beautiful brunette as I spear my fingers through her hair.

The flight attendant comes out. "Can I get you blankets or pillows?"

"Both, thanks."

He leaves, and a moment later, comes out with them and gives them to me. All while Greta sleeps beside me, I situate us so we're laying down together. After I cover us with the blanket. It takes a bit, but I finally fall asleep.

Greta curls up next to me, watching *Stranger Things* on my iPad. I stroke a hand up and down her arm as I hug her close.

Bruno sits down across from me. "Ahem… what's up, brother?" He looks at me and then at Greta before turning back to me. "I emailed Greta's preference sheet. She hardly put anything on it."

I'm not surprised. She is not high maintenance at all. Hell, when we got to the airport, she grabbed her bag to carry over to the plane. I finally had to take it from her and left it for the crew to grab.

She even introduced herself to the pilots and flight attendants. They all ate it right up, but I can't blame them. Greta just exudes this likability that's genuine, and people can pick up on that.

"Thanks, mate, I appreciate it. I'm looking forward to a little downtime." I pick up my water, taking a drink. "Of course, I have that photo shoot in Greece, but we'll have a week to relax before."

Bruno leans forward and taps Greta on the leg. "Hey, doll, I talked to your sister, Sierra, and she's going to work on a new piece for me right here." He holds out his forearm that's bare.

"That's awesome. She does really good work. Sierra is the one who did this piece." She sticks out her leg and shows him the tattoo that takes up most of her thigh. It's from Peter Pan when he, Wendy, and the kids are flying toward the clock tower.

The detail is amazing and when Bruno reaches out and touches it, I want to reach out and slap him, but I don't because I remind myself that it's just him checking out her ink.

"Wow. This piece is fucking badass." He rubs his hand up and down her thigh. It's non-sexual, but I still don't like it.

I nudge his arm with my foot, and when he looks at me, I see the fucker is doing this on purpose. The bastard winks at me before patting Greta's leg and leaning back in his seat.

She slips her headphones back on and smiles at me before restarting the episode she's watching. By the looks of the kids, I think it's the third season she's watching.

We land in Munich a short while later at a private hangar, and we head from one plane to another. This one is smaller, but we only have an hour flight to Croatia.

Greta's excitement is contagious. Even though we've all taken trips like this a lot, we're all seeing it through her joy. I notice paparazzi by the fence, and I give them a show. She smiles up at me as I pull her into a hug.

"We're almost there. Are you getting excited?" I lean down, kissing her softly on the lips before leading her up the stairs into the jet. This flight is quick, and while we're flying, we drink some champagne.

My buddy Kiki and his girl Simone sit behind us. Bruno's best friend, singer/songwriter, Xavier, is meeting us at the boat. Our plane finally lands, and I'm thankful as fuck because over thirteen hours on a plane is too much.

The pilot comes over the speakers, telling us we're preparing to land. We buckle our seat belts, and Greta slips her hand into mine as we begin our descent. I look out the window and there is not a cloud in the sky.

The plane comes to a stop, and once we're able to, we stand up. I hand Greta her bag and grab my backpack. We're loaded up into a van, and once the luggage is loaded, we head toward the dock.

Her leg bounces the closer we get, making me smile. I place my hand on her leg to stop it. "Are you nervous?"

Greta turns to look at me. "No, I'm just excited." She leans in. "If I forget to tell you, thank you for everything."

Fuck me, I'm in trouble.

# nine

## GRETA

I'm in awe the moment we pull up in front of the yacht. It is massive, or at least massive to me, and reminds me of the boats from Below Deck. We take our shoes off and walk up the plank or whatever it is called, and when we climb up the stairs, it is just like a TV show.

The crew is lined up, and then we introduce ourselves to everyone. Captain Ron reminds me of my dad and Miles. He's super cute and so nice. They hand us champagne and while we drink it, they give us the tour.

The room Jett and I are staying in is freaking beautiful. It's all white, with a bouquet of blush pink roses on the little table. I set my bag on the floor next to the chair. Flopping back on the mattress, I sigh happily.

Jett does the same and I giggle as I look at him. He grabs my hand and brings it to his lips. "Should we go upstairs and get a prime seat for when we take off?" Grabbing my hands, he pulls me off the bed.

I'm still not sure how I ended up here. I mean, I know I said yes, but I'm just a girl from Atlanta. We both take a moment to freshen up before, hand in hand, we head up to meet the others.

Bruno hands us shots of tequila and a lime. Jett brings his lime to my lips and I open my mouth, grabbing the end with my teeth. He gives me a naughty grin before throwing back the shot and grabbing the lime with his teeth.

"Your turn." He opens his mouth, and I hold the lime up to his mouth.

I take my shot. The tequila is smooth but burns as it goes down. Grabbing his face, I pull it down so I can reach his mouth. With my teeth, I scrape the lime. He pulls the rind from his mouth and pulls me into his arms as the yacht starts to move away from the dock.

The wind blows my hair behind me as we start to glide through the water. I lean against the railing and take a second to admire the beauty. I've never seen water so blue. Jett comes up behind me, resting his hands on the railing beside mine.

"I don't think I've ever seen something so beautiful." He rests his chin on my shoulder. "It's almost as beautiful as you."

I turn so I'm facing him and push my sunglasses up on my head. "You sure know how to flatter a girl."

"I meant it. I'm so glad we met."

Oh god, my heart freaking melts. He is so sweet, and I tell him I feel the same. "I'm glad we met too."

The chief stew lets us know that lunch is ready. We head up to the outdoor dining area, and I take the seat that Jett pulls out for me. He takes the seat next to me as they set down platters of sandwiches, salad, and fruit.

I'm not shy and fill my plate because I'm starving. I notice the other women here only take the salad, and that's a shame because this all looks so good. Conversation is halted while everyone eats.

Once they clear our plates, we head back down to the deck, soaking up the sun. The girls haven't been overly friendly with me, but they haven't been rude either. I'm sure it's hard for them to trust people because they have money and are probably used to using them to get what they want.

Bruno has been the nicest to me out of everyone. He reminds me of a combination of Joaquin and Erik.

Xavier is covered in ink like me, so we show off some of our pieces to each other. "Your sisters do good work. Bruno said he's gonna see, I think he said, Sierra. Maybe I ought to give them a call too."

"That'd be awesome. They're all amazing, so whoever you choose will do amazing work." My sisters know their shit.

I'm ready to go in the water, so I excuse myself to go down and get into my bikini. I see they unpacked our bags, which is kind of cool, but kind of weird. My swimsuits are in the same drawer as my underwear and Jett's.

I choose the red with white polka dots. I'm just slipping on the bottoms when hands grab my hips.

"Please don't bend over like that because it's making my dick hard." Jett grinds his erection against my ass

I feel that familiar tingle begin low in my belly. "How is it that you can get me so wet without barely touching me?"

A moan slips from my lips as he reaches around me, rubbing my clit. He nips at my neck, then licks up my neck to my ear. Jett bites my lobe, causing me to yelp, but then moan as he pushes two fingers inside me.

"Let me hear you come. Ride my fingers." His voice is husky as he whispers in my ear.

I grab onto his wrist and hold him against my pussy, as I begin to ride Jett's digits. He turns my face to him and our kiss is a fiery gnashing of lips, teeth, and tongues.

Jett swallows my cries as I begin to come, drenching his finger as my body becomes one giant spasm. I should be worried the other can hear us, but right now, I don't care.

Suddenly, I'm flipped onto the bed and then he's inside me. Jett fucks me with short, hard thrusts that cause me to have aftershocks. It is not long before he buries his face in my neck and begins to fuck me erratically. He begins to come, and I can feel every jerk of his cock inside me.

Once we get our wits about us, we get changed and head up to the deck.

"How did you and Kiki meet?" Turning my head from where I'm lying to look at the platinum-blonde supermodel. I can be quiet around new people, and I'm trying to be better at breaking the ice first.

Simone smiles at me. "Bruno introduced us. They were at a charity function I was speaking at. One look and I was in love." She laughs softly to herself. "We've been together for ten years, and our girls are nine, seven, and three."

She picks up her phone and turns it toward me. "They're beautiful. They look like the perfect combination of both of you." Kiki is a six foot four Samoan with long, wavy brown hair, dark brown eyes, and dark-tanned skin.

"Thank you. They do. All three of them have their daddy wrapped around their little fingers."

We turn to the water when someone hollers. It's Bruno who flies by on a jet ski, with Xavier following. A moment later, Jett and Kiki go by on those surfboards that are motorized. I'll admit, it's like a hot guy extravaganza here.

"Your girls are lucky. I love having sisters. I've got three ready-made best friends, and we'd all do anything for each other. Don't get me wrong, I love my brother to pieces. There is just a special bond with us girls." I shake my head. She probably thinks I'm a dork.

"I have two older brothers, and it's the same."

She turns back to her iPad, and I continue to read an ARC of my brother's new novel coming out at the end of the year.

The woman that came with Xavier got seasick. She took some medicine for it, that was going to knock her out, so she's laying down. I figured he would've stayed with her, but she wanted him to have fun.

I flip onto my stomach and decide to close my eyes, soaking up the sun.

Before my eyes even open, I feel him sit next to my hip. Jett's hand strokes my back, causing goose bumps to pop up all over my body. I finally lift my head and smile up at him.

"I fell asleep."

"Come on, let's go take a nap before dinner." He helps me up and we head down to our room.

Before I can collapse on the bed, Jett throws me over his shoulder.

"What are you doing?" I squeal as he slaps my ass.

He carries me into the bathroom and sets me on the counter.

Nestling himself between my legs, caging me in with his hands resting on the counter. He leans down so we're eye to eye. "You and I are about to break in that shower."

I shiver in anticipation, and then we get very dirty and then very clean.

# ten

## JETT

Rubbing my hands through my hair, I give myself a once-over and then head back into our room. Greta's hair hangs down her back in loose waves. She's wearing a pink halter top romper that shows off her incredible body and her ink.

She turns to look at me, smiling. Fuck, I like her. The sex is the best I've ever had. I'm drawn to her, and I make my way to her. Moving her hair to one side, I lean down, kissing her neck. "You look stunning."

Greta's cheeks turn an adorable shade of pink. "I'm sorry, I don't have anything dressier." She bites her lip and looks away.

I grip her chin, making her look at me. "Don't worry, you'd look good in a paper bag."

She laughs and then leans in, kissing me. "You're funny."

My phone rings, and I see it's Josiah. "If you want to head up, I'm going to talk to my manager."

Greta stands up and then leans down, kissing me one more time. "Have a good chat." She leaves the room, shutting the door behind her.

"What's up, mate?" I greet him as I answer the phone.

"How's it going? Are you sick of her yet?" he says with a laugh.

Yes, that used to be me. Never with the same girl more than one night because I'd get sick of them, but not now. Greta is different. I know it's been a short time, but I like her. "It's going great, bro. She's a lot of fun, and she's getting along with everyone."

"Good, good. The two of you are all over social media. Everyone is going crazy for you and the mysterious tattooed beauty. They all want to know if you've finally found the one. This is perfect, and when you win your first Oscar, you better remember to thank me." He's silent for a moment. "Just don't get attached. I need you focused with your eye on the prize."

"Don't worry, bro. I'm not going to get attached." I rub the ache in my chest. "You know I don't have it in me to commit."

There is a click, and I look at the door. Shit, did she hear? "Mate, I have to go, but we'll chat later."

Josiah sighs. "Right, well, have fun and for the love of God, don't fall in love with her."

I stick my phone on the charger and head up to find everyone. My eyes immediately find Greta. She sits next to Bruno, and when she sees me, she smiles, but even from here, I can tell it's a fake smile.

Fuck, I don't know what to do here. I greet everyone and take the seat next to her. The stewardess brings me a vodka soda. I wrap my arm around her waist and thankfully she leans into me.

Maybe she didn't hear me after all. She turns her head. "Did everything go okay with your manager?"

"Yeah, babe. It was all good. He's going to meet us in Greece for the photo shoot." I kiss her behind her ear. The scent of coconut hits me and makes my mouth water, but for once, I don't maul her.

We all make small talk while we wait for them to tell us it is time for dinner. Hand in hand we make our way toward the table. I pull out her chair for her, my mother would beat my ass if I didn't.

"Bru, when do you start filming?"

He's starring in a football drama. Bruno plays a quarterback who gets hooked on opioids and then how he got his life back together. This is his first starring role, and I'm bloody happy for him.

His smile turns big and bright. "I start training next month, and then we start shooting in two."

"Cheers, bro." I hold up my drink and everyone follows suit.

We all offer him our congratulations, and then they bring our food. They first bring out the salad course. It is full of peppers, cucumbers, tomatoes, and red onion. No one says a word while we all eat.

The rest of the meal is amazing, and the others decide they want to go to a club. Greta says she wants to stay on the yacht, so I decide to stay with her. Normally I'd be all about that party life, but I would rather spend time with her.

After watching the others leave on the tinder, we get settled on the top deck. I ask them to bring us a bottle of champagne and to give us privacy. I'm not going to fuck her out here because people will try to film us so they can sell it. I just want to be alone with her.

"This place doesn't seem real." She leans against my chest, taking a drink of her champagne. "I mean, the water is so blue, it honestly reminds me of your eyes." Greta sighs, shaking her head. "Oh god, that's so corny. I'm sorry."

She doesn't even know what her words do to me. "It is not corny at all. I've never had someone say something like that to me before."

It is the truth. Most of the women I spend my time with only ever talk about themselves and whatever they think I can do for their careers. Annoying, yes, but it's easier to keep it casual that way.

I really need to tread carefully with Greta, but damn, it's going to be hard.

Greta stirs beside me, and I wrap my arm around her, pulling her snug to my chest. I rub my lips against the skin of her upper back. God, this girl has turned me into a goddamn sex addict.

We spent most of last night lying out on the bunny pad, listening to music and making out because I couldn't keep my hands off her. While gazing up at the stars, she asked me about New Zealand and my family.

"I was born and raised in Takapuna, a suburb of Auckland. My mum and dad still live there. He's a retired architect, and she still works as a primary school teacher. My sister Adrienne lives near the university and teaches contemporary dance and choreography." I rolled to my side to face her. "How did you all end up doing the tattoo and piercing thing?"

Greta gave me that gorgeous smile of hers. "Mona was the first, which makes sense since she's the oldest. Anyway, she'd always been artistic. They all are, including our brother Miles." She shrugged. "I'm not sure why I'm the only one that really didn't have some sort of artistic talent or gift."

"I watched some of your makeup videos, and I'd say that probably takes some artistic talent." I pulled her until Greta was on top of me, straddling my hips. The sun was setting behind her and she looked like my tattooed angel.

Once the sky turned an inky black, I helped her up, and we made it back to our room before I was devouring her pussy like I was starved for it.

Now, she sleeps heavily beside me. I wore her out last night. I only snuggle with her for a few more minutes before I ease out of bed and head into the bathroom. After taking care of business, I brush my teeth.

Back in our room, I quickly change into some workout clothes and head to the little workout area. Bruno comes up while I'm using the elliptical.

"Morning, mate. Did you guys have fun last night?"

He scrubs his hands down his face. "Yeah, man, the club was hopping. What did you guys do?"

I laugh when he wiggles his eyebrows at me. "You're a dog."

We spend the next half hour working out. Finishing up, we find a couple of towels and bottles of water waiting for us. Heading down to our rooms, the stewardess tells us when we come up that they'll start serving breakfast.

I find Greta where I left her, passed out in bed. The sheet only covering part of her ass. She looks sexy as hell. Grabbing my phone, I open the camera app and snap a couple pictures of her.

After this ends, I'll have these to remember her by. I hop into the shower to rinse off, and I'm about to step out when arms wrap around me. Placing my hands on top of hers, I feel her lips on my back.

I pull her around so she's in front of me. Her nose and cheeks are pink from being out in the sun and it makes me smile. As much as I want to fuck her, I hear her stomach growl. "Let's go eat, babe."

In our room, she throws on her hot pink booty shorts and black cropped, sleeveless tee. If I could, I'd convince her to wear nothing but her bikini. She needs to show that shit off, but then, of course, part of me doesn't want to share her with anyone.

Up on the deck, Greta and I both ask for coffees and bloody marys. The stewardess stops next to her after handing us our drinks. "At one o'clock, we'll take you to shore. There are lots of places to see, and we've arranged for you to have a nice lunch with a beautiful view of the water. Does that sound good?"

We all agree that it sounds more than great. Chances are we'll get recognized, but people tend to leave us alone. If they take pictures or videos and post them online, that's a good thing. Josiah wanted us everywhere, and it would seem that's what he's getting.

# eleven

## GRETA

There is so much to see, I don't even know where to look. I want to take pictures, but I don't want to miss a single moment. Everyone else is shopping while I take in the beautiful architecture. I believe they said it is called Old Town.

I find myself at the end of the road in front of a church. Looking behind me, I realize that I've wandered away from the group. I take a minute to admire the beauty and take a quick selfie before heading back toward the shops.

Each store I pass, I take a quick peek inside, but I don't see them, so I keep walking. The hair on the back of my neck stands and I freeze. Looking around, I don't see anyone.

Turning to keep walking I slam into a body. "Whoa, babe. Didn't mean to scare ya."

I'm relieved to find Jett in front of me. I smile up at him, shaking my head. "I didn't realize that I had wandered so far away from you guys."

"Yeah, when I didn't see you when I stepped outside, I started to get worried, but then I found you staring behind you. Did you see something?" Jett wraps his arm around my shoulders and leads me toward the rest of our group.

I shake my head. "No, but I just got a weird feeling, that's all."

Jett gives me a squeeze, and then we all head toward the restaurant. I keep myself tucked in close to him because I just noticed a guy across the road from us, and he's taking pictures.

Our group stays close together until we get to Nautika. They seat us outside, with a gorgeous view of the Adriatic. I take a quick video of the restaurant and then the view from our table.

I send it to Nick, my sister Sierra's partner. He's a chef and a restauranter, I'm sure he'll appreciate what I'm seeing.

The waiter hands me a menu once I'm seated next to Jett. We decide to order an assortment of appetizers, and they order a couple of bottles of champagne. Everything is so expensive, and I've tried to give Jett money twice, but both times he told me no.

His exact words were, "I invited you, you're not paying for shit." Then he kissed the crap out of me.

While we eat, they all talk about the various projects they have going on. I feel so out of place right now. They live these amazing lives and I'm just a girl from Atlanta that likes makeup, tattoos, and piercings.

It dawns on me that I don't belong here. Jett was crazy to invite me along. Maybe I should talk to him about this, or maybe I should just suck it up. I guess maybe I'm just intimidated being around these super successful people. Ugh... I want to run and hide.

"Greta?" I look up from my plate at Xavier. "I know you and your sisters own a tattoo studio, but what does your brother do?"

They all turn to look at me, and I'm suddenly nervous. I feel a hand on my thigh, and I know that's Jett giving me his silent support. "Umm... he's an author. His most popular books are his Detective Jameson novels." I quickly pull up his website and hold my phone out to him.

"I've read those," Bruno says from beside him. They're really good. I can't wait for the next one."

I smile widely. "Well... I happen to have an advanced copy of it, and I am sure my brother would tell me you could read it."

He hands me my phone, and I shoot Miles a quick text.

> **Greta:**     Hey brother, I feel like I'm in heaven. Anywho, I'm here with Bruno Nixon and he likes your books. Could I let him read the ARC?

He's up because it immediately goes to "read" The little black dots begin to bounce.

> **Miles:**     Hell yes, he can read it.

My cheeks hurt from grinning so big. I look up at Bruno. "He said, hell yes."

He claps his hands together and holds his hand out. "Can I text him?" The man takes my phone and starts typing out a message. They text back and forth until the next course comes out.

Bruno hands me my phone back. "Your brother is a cool guy."

I nod. "You're not wrong. When we're back on the boat, I'll grab the book for you. If it's possible, I think this is the best one yet. I may be biased though."

He smiles at me, and then we go back to eating. By the time we're done, I'll admit I'm a little drunk, just enough to feel giggly. We have an hour before we have to return to the yacht. We decide to walk the long way back. The Old City is such a beautiful place to see.

The buildings look like they are from a movie. I take lots of pictures and selfies. Simone even stops someone, asking them to take our picture. We all line up at the entrance of the Pile Gate.

Thanks to the buzz I'm rocking, I get into posing with everyone. It's weird knowing that we have an audience. People are aiming their phones at us, well, not me. I still don't know if I could ever get used to it.

Jett grabs me and takes a selfie of us cheek to cheek. I do admit we make a beautiful couple when he shows me the picture he took. He even takes one with my phone of us kissing—like really kissing.

He pulls away and I sway on my feet, making him chuckle. I stick my tongue out at him before he wraps his arm around my neck, kissing my temple. I'm still in shock that he's not shy about the PDA.

"I love that sound you just made," Jett whispers against my ear.

I look up at him, confused. "What sound?"

He smiles that damn movie star smile at me. "When I kissed your temple, you gave a little sigh." He imitates me. "It's fucking beautiful."

Shaking my head, I wrap my arm around his waist. "You're a dork," I tell him as we make our trek toward the dock for the tinder to pick us up.

By the time we get there, the boat is waiting for us. One of the deckhands holds out his hand to help us girls get on, but Jett hops in. I squeal as he grabs me, lifting me on the boat.

Once we're all on, we head back to the yacht.

The sun is warming my skin as I lay on the paddle board while Jett moves us through the water slowly. Today is our last day, we disembark tomorrow. The others are staying one more day, but Jett needs to be in Greece.

God, that sounds so weird to say. I move my hand through the warm water. If my sisters and brother could see me now.

"Babe, you look like a tattooed goddess right now."

My cheeks heat up. Will I ever get used to the things he says to me? "You're good for a woman's ego." I tip my head back and smile up at him. "You know you're not so bad yourself."

His laugh is loud and boisterous. I sit up as he paddles us close to the yacht. There is a boat I can see in the distance. It looks like they're pointing a camera at us. I quickly look away, and once I'm able, I slip into the water.

After I climb out of the water, I head directly down to our room. Locking myself in the bathroom, I flop down on the toilet seat. It feels icky knowing that people have been taking pictures and recording us. I've avoided getting online, scared of what I might see. He's a famous movie star, I'm nothing. People probably wonder what he's doing with me.

*Knock, knock, knock.* "Greta? Open the door, babe."

Taking a deep breath, I stand up and twist the knob. He pushes the door open and pulls me into his arms. "What's wrong? Simone said you looked upset."

I pull back and look up at him. "I don't know if I can do this."

# twelve

## JETT

"I don't know if I can do this." Greta looks at me with tear-filled eyes. "There was someone watching us, taking pictures. I'm not sure I'll ever get used to it."

Fuck, Josiah said the guy wouldn't be a problem, but clearly, the guy was going to do whatever the hell he wants. I really like her, and it has not been a hardship to spend time with her. I'm just not relationship material. In the long run, I'd hurt her, and not on purpose.

I have two choices here. First, I could just send her on her way and thank her for hanging out with me. No harm, no foul, or I could convince her to give this a chance. We could continue to have great sex and see some beautiful places together.

Stroking her cheek with my thumb, I lean down. "I'm sorry, babe. Please don't let them fuck this up. I promise you I'll never let them get close. If it makes you feel better when we're in Greece, I can hire some private security."

Greta worries her lip and shakes her head. My stomach sinks, but then she says softly, "No, please don't do that. I'll be okay."

I smile before leaning in and kissing her deeply. Fuck, I don't think I'll ever get tired of kissing her. Her lips were made for kissing—they're full and soft. I pull my lips away and rest my forehead against hers.

"Thank you, baby. I'm not ready to say goodbye."

She sinks into me and wraps her arms around my waist. Greta yawns widely, and I laugh.

"Let's take a nap before dinner."

We climb on the bed and she curls up next to me, draping her leg over mine. In no time, we're both asleep.

Our flight lands in Zagreb, and we're staying here tonight before we arrive in Greece tomorrow early evening. This flight was only an hour, thankfully. At least once we're in Greece, we'll have a week to relax before my shoot.

I will have to exercise every day, but I'll do that every morning. Josiah has set up some spa treatments for us and got us a gorgeous villa to stay in. I also told him about the paparazzi freaking Greta out. He promised me he'd warn the guy about getting too close. If Greta gets spooked again, there is a chance that she could split.

Once we're able to get off the plane, I grab our bags, leading her down the stairs and to the waiting limo. The driver takes our bags from me, placing them in the trunk while we get settled inside.

"Tonight, we'll order room service and just relax," I tell her as I wrap my arm around her.

She yawns. "That sounds freaking amazing." Snuggling into me, Greta kisses the underside of my chin. "I know I've said it before but thank you for an amazing time."

"Stop thanking me. I've had an amazing time too."

We get checked in, and they lead us up to our suite. It's small, but we're only here tonight. Tomorrow we'll finally be in Santorini, and it'll be nice to settle in one place for a few a bit.

I place our bags on the chaise lounge next to the window. Greta flops back onto the mattress. Not one to miss an opportunity, I run and jump, straddling her. Pinning her arms above her head.

"I couldn't resist."

"Well, what are you going to do with me?" Her chest rises and falls rapidly, and she licks her lower lip.

I lean down until we're chest to chest. "Oh, I can think of a few things." Then I go about wearing her out before we take a nap.

I'm not sure what time it is when I wake up, but I find I'm in bed alone. Greta's voice drifts in from the patio. I make my way out to her but pause in the doorway when she says my name.

"He's being very good to me." She smiles and listens to whoever is on the other end. "What is going on with Heidi? I can't get a hold of her." Greta spots me and smiles at me. "Mona, I talk to her every day. Is she mad at me?"

I sit down, pulling her onto my lap, and rubbing a hand up and down her thigh.

"Please tell her to call me. I'll let you guys know when we arrive in Greece." She pauses and nods, which is cute, since they can't see her. "Okay, tell everyone I love them. Bye, Mo."

"How's your family? Is everything okay with Heidi?" I know that she's the youngest of Greta's siblings.

"They're all good, and Mona says Heidi's fine, but it's weird she's not answering me."

I wrap my arms around her and hug her. "I'm sorry, darling."

We stay curled up in the chair, watching the sunset until Greta finally speaks. "The guy who broke her heart in high school is back in the picture and I guess I'm not sure where they're at, but we've never gone this long without talking."

Her stomach growls, making me chuckle.

"Let's order some food."

She grabs the room service menu inside the room and starts looking it over. I order a fish dish, while Greta orders pasta.

When it arrives, we eat in bed, leaning up against the mountain of pillows. I can't remember the last time I ate a meal kicked back like this, but I like it. It isn't long before we're done eating and getting ready for bed.

She's asleep the moment her head hits the pillow. It is creepy, I know, but I just take a second to watch her. With Greta, I'm starting to crave things I never wanted in my life. I figured I would be a bachelor for the rest of my life, but Greta's got me confused.

I reach out and push her hair back from her face, she sighs and then snuggles into the bed. After stripping down to my boxer briefs, I climb into bed too. It's like she can sense me lying next to her, because she rolls over and scoots in close to me.

Greta has turned me into a snuggler and I'm not sure how I feel about that. I just have to remind myself that this is temporary, it'll be over in a few weeks, and I'll go back to doing what I do best... love 'em and leave 'em.

Why doesn't that sit right with me?

# thirteen

## GRETA

I stare out the window in wonder as we take off from the Zagreb airport. There are so many beautiful things to see. It is a shame that we were only here for a day. I'm just glad that once we get to Greece, we'll be there for two weeks. I need a break from traveling.

I smile to myself thinking how hoity-toity I sound. I've never seen so many beautiful places. No matter what happens with Jett, I'll never regret this because look at what I've gotten to see. Getting to know the real Jett, the one that isn't plastered all over the tabloids.

His hand rests on my thigh as he sleeps beside me. Flying private has been a fun experience, and not having to deal with busy airports has been a big plus. This flight is only four hours, thankfully.

I might as well get some rest too. Leaning my seat back, I snuggle into Jett's side and immediately fall asleep.

"Beautiful?" I hear someone say softly. "Honey, wake up. We're almost there."

Sitting up, I stretch my arms up above my head. I smile at Jett and then turn to look out the window. "Wow," I whisper.

The water looks like sapphires sparkling in the sun. I feel Jett lean against my back, looking out the window, and seeing what I am. The pictures I've seen of Santorini don't do it justice. The sun shines bright on the white structures, some with bright blue roofs.

"It doesn't look real," I whisper quietly, not hiding the awe in my voice.

He kisses my temple. "It doesn't, does it."

We slip our sunglasses on as we stand up to disembark the plane. The flight attendant stands by the door as we move toward it. Jett gives her a chin lift and I give her a smile. "Thank you so much."

It is bright and hot as we head down the stairs to the waiting SUV. "I keep pinching myself, thinking this can't be real." I bounce in my seat. I'm filled with a childlike wonder of the beauty around me. "I've never been here before, and I'm excited to do some exploring."

We pull up in front of Echoes Luxury Suites. I can't help but gasp because it is the most beautiful place. He helps me out of the SUV, and I keep hold of his hand as we head inside.

"Mr. Hamilton. Welcome to Echoes. We have a beautiful suite for you and your lovely wife."

Jett squeezes my hand and winks at me before dragging me to our room for the next week. I guess it is not technically a room. When I step inside, I can't believe it. Everything is white, minimalistic, and beautiful. The manager shows us around, and I stop in front of the double doors in our bedroom, seeing that we have an infinity pool.

"We'll be able to set up your meals out here if you choose to stay in," he says. "We have a beautiful spa, with treatments already set up for you, whenever you choose. Your manager also arranged for a wine tasting."

He starts walking toward the door. "Please let me know if there is anything I can do for you to make you both more comfortable."

"Thanks, bro." Jett hands him money, and then he disappears. He turns to look at me. "Do you believe this place?" Stalking toward me, I feel some warmth in my belly. "I'm going to enjoy fucking you in that pool," he whispers into my ear before nipping at the tender flesh.

Jett leaves me to freshen up in the bathroom, and I step out of our room, taking videos with my phone. God, it is like a little slice of heaven here. We swap places and, in the bathroom, I wash my face, brush my teeth, and then moisturize.

I step out of the bathroom and grab a bottle of water from the fridge. After twisting off the cap, I take a huge swig, sighing as the cool water slides down my throat.

Jett's out by the water, talking on his cell phone. While he does that, I take a minute to try Heidi.

"Hey, big sissy."

Thank god, she finally answered me.

"Sorry I've been silent. Colton and I are figuring things out and have been spending a lot of time together."

I nod, although she can't see me. "No worries, I was just concerned about you. We've never gone this long without talking."

"I know, again, I am sorry. How's your little adventure anyway? You two have been all over social media and people love you guys, but just be careful. They can be relentless and he's got a reputation."

"I'm being careful, I promise. Jett even offered to hire private security to protect us if needed. I love you, little sissy."

She disconnects after some more small chat, and I feel better now that I've heard her voice.

Jett comes inside and pulls me into his arms. "Why don't we walk around and see if we can find someplace to eat."

"That sounds great." I slip on my sandals, and then we head out.

I follow behind Jett and Josiah, feeling like the third wheel. I'm not even sure they know I'm here. This part of the trip started so magical, and then once Josiah got here, the magic died.

The first two days, we didn't stray far from our suite. Sure, we left to eat, but other than that, we stayed in our room or outside in the pool. My brown hair is starting to look blonde from the sun, and my skin is dark tan, even though I've been putting sunscreen on.

We did sightsee the day before yesterday. Jett arranged for a private tour for us...

Stepping outside, I smile at Jett because there is a scooter and a man standing next to it. He holds two helmets for us. "Mr. Hamilton, we've got your tour programmed into this GPS." He holds up what looks like an iPhone. "We've got several great sites for you to see."

Jett shakes his hand, and then he disappears down the road. He hands me my helmet and we both stick ours on. Once he climbs on, he holds his hand out to me. I've never been on one before, but I trust him to be careful.

For a while, we just drive around. There is something freeing about being on a bike with the wind blowing through your hair. We start a trek around the island, looking at each of the beautiful churches.

We don't stop long enough to get off the scooter. There are tourists everywhere and so far no one has recognized him, and we're trying to keep it that way.

Jett turns off the scooter when we reach Profitis Ilias Monastery. We climb off and he grabs my hand after hanging our helmets off the handlebars.

"This place is stunning." I smile up at him.

"Not as stunning as you."

I slap at his chest as he gives me a wink. "Oh brother, that was cheesy."

He drags me toward the door. God, I love the sound of his laugh—it's deep and rich. It sounds like it comes from deep inside his chest. We were greeted by a guide who gives us a tour.

The chapel is gorgeous. The walls are the canvas for the paintings. There are silver candelabras everywhere. I'm not a very religious person, but I do feel a peace wash over me as I stand here.

Jett wraps his arm around my waist and gives me a squeeze. Does he feel it too? The guide takes us to another room that is covered in pictures. The flooring is old, dark planks. You can just smell the history.

He leads us to a door that leads us outside, where there are little stands. They're selling homemade items. I buy a ceramic painting of a sunset. Our guide leaves us and we stroll along the stone path.

We stop, taking a second to enjoy the beauty of the water. It's picturesque and Jett takes a selfie of us, with the water at our back. He looks at his phone and then turns it toward me.

"We look good together."

"I couldn't agree more." I grip his face and pull it down to mine, kissing him thoroughly. "Ughh... I like kissing you."

He wraps his arms around me. "You say it like it's a bad thing."

I slap his ass, laughing as I start to jog away from him, but it becomes a shriek as he runs after me. There are people everywhere, and I forget all about them when he catches me around the waist, spinning me around and around.

"Sta-ahp." I laugh-scream.

Jett grabs my hand and we make our way toward the parking lot. He climbs on the scooter, with me getting on behind him, and we take off. We're doing a wine tasting tonight, and they're pairing food with each wine.

Since neither of us has dressy clothes, we're heading to a boutique to get something to wear. I just hope I find something cute within my budget because I'm definitely not going to let him buy me something. Jett has already done too much. How would I ever be able to thank him?

# fourteen

## JETT

I sip my tequila as I stand outside, waiting for Greta so we can go to the wine tasting or pairing. As I stare out at the blue water in the distance, I'm filled with guilt. I really like her, and once she finds out what I did, she'll hate me, but if I make it worth her while, maybe it'll soften the blow.

When I think back to all the other women, there is not a single one that I would still want to hang out with. Not until Greta and that makes this whole situation shittier.

Turning when I hear footsteps, I almost swallow my tongue. At the boutique earlier, she wouldn't let me see the dress she picked out. While she was trying it on, I gave the girl my card and told her to give Greta whatever she wanted.

She was pissed, but then I kissed her right there in front of the salesclerk. While Greta was in a daze, I led her outside. Once we got back here, I took a shower first.

I'm wearing light sand color linen pants and a button-up shirt with short sleeves. I slowly take her in. Her dress is a lavender halter top and flared skirt. It hits her mid-thigh and showcases her long legs and tattoos.

She chose gold gladiator sandals. Her hair is up in an intricate ponytail. In other words, she is a fucking goddess.

"Do I look okay?" Greta does a little spin.

A groan slips past my lips when I get a look at the back of her dress. It's open to the base of her spine. Fuck, I'd rather just keep her to myself. "You're a vision." I pull her into my arms and kiss her softly.

I've never been one to show affection and I have never been a fan of PDA, and I know Josiah told me to sell it. That's what I was doing at first, but she's becoming an addiction.

I grab her hand, and we head out to the waiting car. The vineyard is on the other side of the island. Looking behind me, I notice the photographer following us from a distance. My stomach turns, and I face forward, wrapping my arm around Greta's shoulder, and hug her into my side.

She's none the wiser and leans into me. Once we pull up to the winery, I help her out.

The owner, Yiannis, greets us as we step inside. "Mr. Hamilton. Welcome, welcome. It is our pleasure to have you here with us." He grabs Greta's hand and brings it to his lips, kissing the back of it.

If he wasn't an old man, I'd have been pissed. Although I still don't like it, which is troubling. I've never cared about stuff like that. I don't get jealous. I have no reason to.

We take a tour of the vineyard and I'm honestly bored as shit. The only thing I like about wine is drinking it. I'll admit I do love watching Greta. She's got her arm through Yiannis's and is giving him her rapt attention. The old man is eating it up.

I have my phone out when he says something to her. She throws her head back, laughing. I quickly snap a picture and take a quick video of her. Before I can stop myself, I post the picture on my social media.

I'm not sure what to write, so I simply put, *"My Girl"* with a heart emoji. Thirty seconds after I post it, my notifications start going haywire. Thankfully my phone is on silent, so I shove it into my back pocket.

The spot we're seated at is overlooking the vineyard. It is gorgeous, and when I look across the table, I freeze. Greta is looking at it with a tear leaving a silvery trail down her cheek.

"Hey, baby, are you okay?"

She gets up and comes around to me, sitting on my lap. "Seriously. Thank you for asking me to come. This has been the most fun I've ever had." Greta hugs me tight, burying her face in my neck.

Fuck, my heart races in my chest. My stomach does a weird dip and the little voice inside my head tells me to run. Instead, I hug her tightly. "Stop thanking me, darling. It has not been a hardship spending time with you."

Greta pulls back to look at me, and I reach up, brushing her tears away. She gives me a watery smile and I keep her right where she's at when Yiannis comes out. "I would like to choose your wine and food if you'd let me."

I nod. "That sounds great, mate."

He leaves us, and I wrap my arms back around her.

"I have never met a woman like you, Greta Collins." Kissing her neck, I sigh. "I cannot wait to get back to our suite. Make sure you eat enough because you're going to need your energy."

Her cheeks flush the most beautiful pink, and she bites her lower lip, letting me know she likes that idea. This wine pairing better get over quick.

Gripping Greta's hips, she rocks slowly on top of me. I'm sitting on the bench in the pool and she's straddling me. My cock is buried deep inside her pussy and after fucking her two other times since we've been back, you'd think my dick would be spent.

Instead, it lets me know it is DTF at all times around her. She got a little drunk. Hell, I did too. The moment we were in the suite, I had her against the wall, her panties off, and my cock inside her.

The second time was on the bed, while we were supposed to be changing into our swimsuits.

Once we got into the pool, Greta rested her arms on the edge of the pool. She was bathed in moonlight, and before I could stop myself, I was behind her. It started out with just some heavy make-out stuff and quickly became what we're doing now.

Luckily our pool is hidden enough that no one will see us. I'm inside her as deep as I can go, and she does little circles with her hips. Even in the water, I can feel how hot and how wet she is.

She's strangling my dick as I begin to rub her clit. Greta grabs my face, attacking my mouth like she is starving for me. Our tongues duel and the minute she begins to come, I swallow her cries and begin thrusting up into her. That tingle at the base of my spine begins, and in no time, I begin to come violently inside her.

I hold Greta down as I press up. Letting go, I reach between us and grab one of her nipple rings. I give it a little tug, and my dick twitches inside her as she milks every drop of cum out of me. She pulls her face away from mine, panting quietly. She wraps her arms around my head, hugging me to her breasts.

"Fuck, I can't get enough of you," I mutter against her skin before licking between her breasts. "I'm going to need a little bit of recovery time and a nap." Reluctantly pulling her off me, we climb out of the water.

I wrap one of the robes around her and throw on the other. We are both so exhausted that we collapse on the bed, curl up together, and fall asleep.

# *fifteen*

## GRETA

While Jett and Josiah walk ahead of me, it occurs to me that there is something about the other man that I don't trust. I'm not sure what it is, and he certainly hasn't done anything to me, but he just gives off this weird, sketchy vibe.

Right now, we're on our way to have lunch, and then they're going to have a Zoom meeting with a casting director and director for some film that Jett has been hoping to get a call about.

We reach the little café, and they step inside ahead of me and let the door swing shut before I can step inside. I pull open the door and find them already taking a seat at a table.

Jett at least stands when I approach and pulls the chair out for me. We order drinks and then just some cheese, meat, and bread. They talk about Jett's upcoming schedule and the cologne ad he'll be shooting.

Apparently while I have been sleeping, he's been out running or working out. I do notice when our food comes that he avoids the bread, but he does ask for some extra veggies.

I scan my phone while they talk. Checking my social media, I see that I'm tagged in several posts. Each one is a picture of Jett and me all around Santorini. Online, I type our names into the search bar.

There are people speculating how quickly he'll break up with me. A couple that are calling us the new "*it*" couple, and will we make it. I close out everything and set my phone down.

I munch on some carrots dipped in hummus when I feel Jett's hand on my thigh, giving it a squeeze. Placing mine on his, I give him one in return. It helps me relax and just know that he's in work mode I can't fault him for that. He takes his acting career seriously.

Jett holds my hand as we head back to our suite. He leaves Josiah outside and pulls me into his arms. "I'm sorry. This is just really important."

"Of course, it is. This is your career, and while you do what you need to, I'm going to put on my bikini and lay by the pool."

He kisses me deeply, lots of tongue and groping.

I sway toward him, and he laughs at me, cocky ass. He kisses me one more time, but it's too quick, and then he's gone.

In the bedroom, I strip out of my clothes and put on my bikini. Throwing my hair in a high ponytail, I then rub sunscreen all over my body. My cell phone rings in the other room.

It's Miles. "Hey, big brother." Of course, he's only ten months older.

"Hey, my sister. How's it going?"

I grab my sunglasses and head outside. "It's good. Jett's with his manager, so I'm going to lay out by the pool."

"Have you been online?"

I sigh. "Yeah, I have. It's so weird that people care who he's dating. We've had people follow us around, and he offered to hire private security. That's not necessary, no one gets too close." The only people that have approached him was a few people asking for an autograph or a picture.

"Just be safe and call me if you need me."

God, I love him… obviously, but he's a good guy, and I don't say that just because he's my brother. "I will. How's Victoria?"

She's Mona's man's cousin. The moment she met my brother, she was smitten, and he felt the same.

"She's great. We're getting ready to head to New York. Don't tell anyone, but I'm going to propose to her," he says quietly. She must be there.

"That is fantastic news. I love her so much for you. I'd be honored to call her my sister." My cheeks hurt from smiling widely. "When I get home, we'll have to have a party to celebrate."

Before we hang up, he promises to send pictures after he does it. I set my phone in the one little shade spot before lying down on the platform, right over the water of the pool. Once I lay my towel down, I get on my stomach, resting my head on my arms.

It is so hot today, so every so often I slide off into the water, floating on my back. Dipping my head back, I get my hair completely saturated and slicked back. I swim over to the wall and rest my arms on it, again taking in the beauty because how can I not.

Getting back on the platform, I lay on my back for a little while. Grabbing my phone, I check to see if Jett texted me or anything, but I can see he hasn't. Who knows how long those meetings can go. I decide to order myself some room service, and while I wait for it to come, I quickly take a shower.

I'm dressed, and my hair is dried before my food arrives. She sets it on the little table right outside.

"Thank you so much."

The woman smiles and nods before leaving.

Jett didn't say what the plan was for dinner, so I'm eating light. I sit down, digging into the Greek salad I ordered. God, I think this is the best salad I have ever had. The veggies are fresh and crisp. It's so good, I eat the whole thing. Back inside, I place my baklava on the counter in the little kitchenette. That'll be a good snack for later.

Checking my phone, I don't see any missed texts or calls. I crawl onto the bed and snuggle in. It takes me no time until I fall asleep.

I moan as my eyes pop open. It takes a second to register that Jett is between my legs, eating my pussy with vigor. He grabs my piercing and gives it a tug, making me cry out. Grabbing his head, I begin to fuck his mouth as he finger fucks me.

My orgasm catches me off guard, and I come with a shot. Instead of stopping, he keeps sucking my clit and hits that spot deep inside me. "Stop. I can't take anymore." I moan, but that pressure builds. "Oh god, oh shit. Fuck, fuck, fuck." My eyes roll back in my head, my ears ring, and I swear I black out.

Jett finally brings me down and then kisses his way up my body. He kisses me deeply before maneuvering us so we're laying chest to chest. "Don't you want to have sex?"

He smiles and nods. "I do, but I'm beat, and I just want to hold you. Plus, when I got back and saw you, I suddenly got really hungry."

I can taste myself on his lips as he leans forward, kissing me.

"You're such a charmer." I snuggle in close, and in no time, we're both out.

Sitting by the water, I take a sip of the champagne I ordered an hour ago. Jett and I were supposed to go to dinner two hours ago, but he went over to speak to Josiah, and I haven't heard from him since.

I texted him once, but I don't want to seem needy, so I don't text him back even though I want to. This is the third night that I have been alone. Sure, we spend time during the day together, but tonight I'll be by myself again.

I forgo the glass and just drink the champagne straight out of the bottle. It's pathetic I know, but if I wanted to hang out by myself, I'd rather be at home. Inside, I carry the champagne into the bedroom.

Because I have a buzz and I'm dumb, I get online and see what's being said about us now. My stomach pitches because there's a picture from the day we went to lunch, and I was walking behind them. The headline says, "Trouble in paradise already?" Others said something similar.

My sisters have all texted or tried to call me, but I honestly don't know what to say. If I go home, am I giving up on something that could be life changing? What if he's the one, but I walk away before I get the chance to find out?

A ping sound has me picking up my phone.

> **Jett:** Hey gorgeous, what are you doing?

I quickly type out a response.

> **Greta:** Drinking. I add the emoji of the face sticking its tongue out.

The black dots start to bounce.

> **Jett:** Be downstairs in ten minutes. I'm sending a car to pick you up and bring you to me. I'm sorry I kept you waiting.

I shouldn't be irritated, and he did say sorry. This was technically part of a working trip for him.

> **Greta:** Okay, see you soon.

I get off the bed and grab one of my rompers, laying it on the bed. In the bathroom, I brush my teeth and add a little bronzer to my face. My tan is top-notch. Miles, me, and Dad are the only ones that really tan, it's great.

My hair is in little braids and twists, and then in another braid. Once I get my gladiator sandals on and then head to the front.

The car pulls up, and he gets out. "Ms. Collins?"

"Yes, that's me."

He holds the door open for me, and I climb inside. Fifteen minutes later, we're pulling up to a restaurant that looks like it has an amazing view.

The driver opens the door for me and holds his hand out.

"Thank you," I say as I stick mine in his.

He leaves the car right in front and leads me to the outdoor seating area. Jett spots me and stands as we approach. Handing the man money, he dismisses him and grabs my hand, pulling me toward him.

Jett kisses me softly. "Hi, gorgeous. Come sit." He leads me to the table.

Josiah stands and comes around to me. "Greta, you are stunning." He kisses both cheeks, and I try not to gag because he lingers a little too long for my taste. It gives me the willies.

I take a seat, and Jett sits next to me. He places his hand on my thigh, stroking the skin with his thumb.

He looks at his phone and then at us. "I have a meeting that's been rescheduled twice, and they can chat now. You two, enjoy your evening."

Once he leaves, Jett leans in. "I missed you today."

That makes me smile. "I missed you too. Sorry about the champagne. I was bored and drowning my sorrows."

"I know. I'm sorry that I've been so busy since Josiah got here. That was not planned at all." He grabs my hands. "If you want to go home, I'll arrange everything."

He's giving me an out, but I know deep down that I want to continue this adventure. I'm falling for him, hard. Does he feel the same about me? The only way to figure this all out is to spend more time with him. I shake my head. "I don't want to go home. This is all for your career, it's no hardship to hang out alone in

Greece."

"Tomorrow, we head to the location for the photo shoot and ad. I want you there with me." Our server takes our drink order, and Jett orders us some appetizers. Once he's gone, he turns back to me. "I am sorry that I've abandoned you the past few days."

I shake my head. "Stop apologizing. I'm here now, and we're going to enjoy our food and drinks."

Like he could read my mind, the server comes to deliver our drinks. Jett holds up his glass, and I do the same. "To an amazing end to an amazing trip."

We clink our glasses together and then dig into the food they just delivered.

# sixteen

## JETT

Greta curls up next to me and nuzzles under my chin. "Did you always want to be an actor?" She kisses right over my heart.

I wrap my arm around her, hugging her into my side. "Through school, I actually wanted to play rugby professionally. I was really good, but I blew out my knee in secondary school, or high school, and I just couldn't play like I used to. I was on vacation in Australia when an agent approached me. I figured I'd do some photos, and that would be it. People refused to believe I could make it, but I proved them wrong every chance I could."

"What is your favorite project you've worked on?"

Smiling in the dark that is the easiest question to answer. "*Redo*. That was the first movie where I got to do a lot of my own stunts. After that movie, I started getting offered better roles."

"That's a good movie. You were really good in it." She kisses the underside of my chin. "I can't believe you did a lot of the stunts yourself. If you weren't acting, what do you think you'd be doing?"

"Hmm… I honestly have no clue. I hated school, growing up, and fucked around. Honestly, acting gave me some direction, I mean, I've still fucked around, but I have a clear path now."

Greta pushes up on her elbow. "What's the path you want to take?"

"Easy. I want to make a film that I'm every part of the process. I want to help write it, act, and direct it."

"A triple threat, I like it." Her breathing starts to slow, and in seconds, she's asleep.

I roll us so her back is to my front and hold her close. I lied to her earlier at dinner, yes, I was working some, but most of the time, I was hanging out at Josiah's place. The truth is I was spooked because I realized how much I was starting to like her.

My plan earlier had been to send her home, but I just couldn't do it. I tried to give her an out and then I wouldn't feel like a dick, but I was fucking glad that she wanted to stay, even though I know it's just going to hurt worse when it's over. Every morning when I get up to go work out Greta moans, grabs my pillow, and hugs it. She looks fucking adorable, and I want to turn right back around and climb back in bed with her.

She's making me feel shit, and that's not what this was supposed to be. I should've told Josiah to fuck off when he came up with the idea. Even if I wanted a relationship with her, how would it even work. This all started on a lie, not her, but me, and I can't not tell her. She'll hate me. Plus, there's just the little fact that I live in LA, and she lives in Atlanta.

I'm just going to enjoy my time with her and hope it doesn't all blow up in my face.

The villa we're staying at is huge, It's got nine bedrooms and eleven bathrooms. The infinity pool in the back is huge, and where some of the shoot is happening.. Thankfully everyone has been friendly to Greta, which has made things easier because then it's not awkward for her. Of course, now sharing a place with others, I can't fuck her like I want. We could always sneak off somewhere if we were desperate.

In the dining room, I find George, the photographer, talking to Greta.

She smiles at me and holds her hand out. "Baby, come here. See what George has planned." Smiling at the other man, she loops her arm through his like they're old friends. "These are gorgeous and you're going to look amazing."

"Your girl has a fabulous eye, Jett." He looks between the two of us. "We're going to get everything set up. I won't see you for a couple of hours. We already know the setup to have the sun working for us."

He and his team leave us to go get everything ready. "I'm going to run on the treadmill and lift until it's time to get in the makeup chair. Do you want to come with?"

"I was thinking about laying down for a bit. I'm exhausted."

She woke me up early this morning with her mouth wrapped around my cock. That led to a morning fuck that was out of this world. We came at the same time and collapsed into a sweaty heap.

"Go rest, and I'll be up in a bit." I kiss her and slap her ass as she turns to walk away.

Greta yelps before disappearing around the corner, and then I head to the gym. I don't want to be too exhausted because I know that part of the shoot is me swimming and then coming out of the water. I just want to get a little bit of a pump.

I run for five miles and then I do some lighter than normal weights. By the time I'm done, I'm a sweaty mess. Upstairs in our room, I find her asleep, so I take a quick shower. I don't bother with my hair or anything because they'll style it how they want.

My phone rings as I wrap my towel around my waist. It's my mum, and I've avoided her calls long enough.

"Hey, Mum. How're you?"

"How are you? That's all you can say after avoiding my call for a week?" Here comes the guilt. "I know my son is a big-time Hollywood star, but I am still your mum."

Rolling my eyes, I tip my head back, looking at the ceiling. She's such a goof, but I love her.

"I am assuming you have questions about Greta. Let's get on with it." I say with a laugh.

"Oh, you're so mouthy." Mum laughs good-naturedly. "She's very beautiful. Is it serious?"

Fuck, I don't want to lie to Mum, but she'd have my ass if she knew the truth.

"I'm not sure yet. She's different than any woman I've met in a long time. She owns a business with her sisters, she's sweet, and doesn't care that I'm Jett Hamilton, the actor."

"I'm happy for you. Just please be careful." She is quiet for a minute. "It is nice to see positive things about you online for a change, ay."

I know my behavior in the past has been a cause of concern. Am I proud of it? Of course not, but I can't change the past. Fuck, since I've met Greta, I've settled down tremendously, not intentionally. It's also been two weeks, and I've behaved longer than that before.

"I know, Mum."

"You've always been wild, you're just like your uncle."

Dad's little brother, John, was wild until his forties, now he's married with a couple of little girls that have him wrapped around their fingers. He's still wild, it's just different now.

Greta stirs and then pushes herself up, looking sleepy and cute. "Mum, I have to let you go. It's time for me to get ready for the photo shoot."

"I want to FaceTime with you and meet her."

Of course, she does.

"Good luck, and we're planning a trip to America for the holidays. I'll talk to Josiah about your schedule. I love you."

"Love you, too." I set my phone down and lean in until Greta and I are eye to eye. "My mum wants to FaceTime with us so she can see you."

"What," she squeals. Shaking her head, she looks up at me. "We don't have to do that if you don't want.

I mean, we haven't really talked about what this is." Greta holds her hands up. "No pressure, I swear."

I push her back on the bed and climb over her. "You and I are a thing. I like you and you like me. We're seeing where this goes."

She smiles and pulls me down to kiss me. "Okay."

While she's freshening up, I throw on some basketball shorts. She comes out and then we head downstairs. I find a tall, light-skinned Black man in the kitchen.

He smiles when we enter. "Jett? I'm Jamie. I'll be doing your styling today."

We shake hands.

"This must be Greta. You are gorgeous."

They hug, and she smiles up at him like they've known each other forever. "So nice meeting you. Can I watch while Jett gets ready? I promise not to get in the way."

Jamie throws his arm around her shoulders, and I follow them into the dining room. He has Greta sit in a chair in the corner and pours her a glass of wine. I can only shake my head because people in this industry can sometimes be rude to outsiders.

It's all her though, she just has a welcoming presence about her. She winks at me before taking a sip of her wine while I get ready.

It takes an hour before I am finally ready to start shooting. I had a spray tan, my hair slicked back to give it a wet look and then sprayed with a mixture of some type of oil to make my skin look shiny.

First, it's pictures of me diving into the water, over and over. Then it was rising up out of the water and walking up the incline while pushing my wet hair back. By the time we're done, I'm exhausted.

George shows me some of the shots he took, and they're great. "See, and then we'll add the ad copy here. He signals to open space. Tomorrow we'll be on the water for the video shots. For those, we're going to start around eight in the morning." He checks his phone. "The chef and his team will be here soon."

"Is it safe to swim in the pool?" Greta walks up to us.

"Naí, absolutely. Everything used on Jett is not harmful to the water," he tells her and then we both watch her walk away. "She'd look beautiful on film," the man says, almost like he's talking to himself.

He's not wrong though. I've seen her magazine spreads. She's a natural, and I'm surprised she's not doing it more. George takes off inside the house with his assistant following behind. They have someone taking down everything they used for the photo shoot today.

I head up to our bedroom and find Greta slipping her bikini on. "Damn, baby. You get my dick so hard."

She giggles at me and then gives me a little shove. "I'll meet you down at the pool, pervert." Shaking her ass as she walks her cute butt out the door.

Wanting to get the oil off my skin, I jump in the shower, scrubbing myself raw to get it all off. The shit we go through for our careers. Once I'm out, I head outside, finding Greta floating around the pool on a giant inflatable raft.

"You look nice and relaxed."

"I am." She's got her eyes closed, and she uses her hand to move her around the water. "Are you going to join me, or are you just going to stand there and stare?"

"I think I might just keep staring. I like what I'm looking at." I jump in, splashing her.

Greta rolls off the raft and then dunks me. We play around in the pool like I used to as a kid. It feels good, freeing. Usually it's parties, drinking, and fucking, but I've loved the time I've spent with her.

Josiah has voiced his concerns that I'm falling for her. He wants me focused on my career and making it to the next level. She's a distraction, or at least that is what he said, but damn, he's the one that came up with the plan.

Greta pulls my attention to her when she swims close, wrapping her arms and legs around me.

"My own personal spider monkey," I tease.

Greta lets go and pushes the top of my head until I go under, but this time I'm ready and I take her down with me. She swims toward me and then leans in, kissing me softly, and then smiles at me while we are both under the water.

Damn, how am I supposed to let her go?

# seventeen

## GRETA

"Hey, Mom. How are you?" I lay back on the lounge chair as I hold my cell phone to my ear. I knew I needed to let everyone know that things are good, great in fact, but I have been so busy. Yesterday we were out on the water all day.

Poor Jett did take after take swimming under water. I could tell that he was getting tired and crabby. He was also starting to get quiet, just doing what was asked of him and nothing more. Afterward, when we got back to the house, they had food waiting for us.

He scarfed his lunch so fast I am not sure he even chewed it. Jett went up to bed and promptly passed out. Jamie and I went shopping so I could buy gifts for Iris and Max and one for Sierra and Nick's baby girl, Ember. Gosh, there are so many babies in the family and it's only going to grow.

Why could I picture a little ornery boy who is wild like his daddy, or that he looks just like Jett. Those thoughts caused my heart to race and the butterflies in my belly to take flight.

"Greta?"

Oh shit, I forgot I was on the phone with my mom. "Sorry. How are you doing?"

She sighs. "We're good, honey. Your sisters have been worried about you. You've been all over online. Most of it's really good, but we've seen some not-so-good stuff."

"I know it's taking some getting used to, but Jett said it should die down once people are used to seeing us together. We're safe, I promise," I stress, but she's Mom, and I can't make her not worry.

"Good, my girl looks so beautiful. You do look good together, I will say that. Is he as wild as they say?"

"Thank you, and no, Mom, he isn't. I think the media just tries to make him look bad. He's been so good to me, and he shows respect to me and anyone he encounters. Thanks to him, I've had such an amazing time," I tell her with conviction.

"Please text or call your sisters or Miles and let them know you're doing good, okay?"

Before hanging up, I tell her I love her, promising to do what she's asked. Setting my phone down, I lie back and close my eyes.

A shadow falls over me, and I open my eyes to find Josiah standing by my hip. "Hey, um... what's up?" I ask as I push myself up into a sitting position. God, this guy gives me a weird vibe.

"Nothing. I just came to give Jett an update on a few things." He looks toward the house. "Is he up?"

I stand up and he follows me inside. Jett comes walking into the kitchen. He just got up because his hair has got that sexy messy look. The gray shorts he's wearing sit low on his hips, showing off the V that he's got, and leaving little to the imagination in the dick region.

As soon as he sees me, he comes toward me and pulls me into his arms. "Why'd you let me sleep so long?" He kisses my neck and then my lips.

"Yesterday wore you out. You needed your rest."

He gives me a look I can't decipher, but it makes my stomach feel all squishy and my heart beat faster. "Thank you for looking out for me." Jett kisses me one more time before he turns to Josiah.

"What's up, mate?" They share a backslapping hug.

"I have some news. The finished script should be here tomorrow."

Jett's smile is huge, and he gives a whoop. He picks me up in his arms, spinning around, making me laugh. Once he sets me down, we turn to face Josiah. The look on his face bothers me, but just as quick as it's there, it is gone.

"That's great, mate. When do I need to audition?" He gives me a squeeze before pouring himself a cup of coffee and then hands me one that's doctored just the way I like it.

Josiah looks at his phone. "You'll need to be ready next month. There are four of you reading for the part of Grayson. I've arranged a meeting with Kim"— my agent—"when you get back."

"Thanks for looking out for me, always."

Jett walks him out, and I'm kind of relieved the guy is gone. While they're outside talking, I head up to our room, stripping out of my bikini. In the nude, I walk into the en suite. My hair is already up, so I step inside the glass shower.

The ceiling with the waterfall showerhead is all stone, along with the wall with the faucet and normal showerhead. I stand under the hot spray, letting the water ease my sore muscles. Hearing the door open and close, my heart starts to race.

Hands wrap around my waist, and they slide up to my chest until they reach my nipple rings. He gives them a tug as he kisses the back of my neck.

"Fuck, you're sexy," Jett whispers against my ear.

I turn in his arms, his erection pressed into my belly. His eyes darken to a navy blue as he looks down at me. My stomach dips and my legs quake. Suddenly my hair is down and he's pressing me into the cold glass.

The minute I gasp, his mouth descends on mine. Jett's lips demand possession of mine. The moment his tongue brushes mine, he growls into my mouth. There is no foreplay. He just lifts my leg, lines up his cock, and thrusts inside me.

My head smacks into the glass, a cry slips past my lips and into his mouth. He pulls back but presses his forehead to mine. Jett holds my eyes and mine begin to burn, his look is intense as he fucks me with abandon.

"What are you doing to me?" he whispers against my lips.

He somehow manages to pull me down hard enough that he's buried impossibly deep inside me, triggering my orgasm. He follows right behind me moaning as he begins to come deep inside me. Panting against my neck, he causes goose bumps to pop up all over my skin.

Once he composes himself, he kisses me behind my ear. "Baby, you continue to blow my mind."

I start giggling like a schoolgirl and kiss his forehead. He pulls out of me and after we quickly wash, we head back into the bedroom. I slip on some blue low-rise panties and a black tank top. Jett throws on some black boxer briefs.

He grabs his phone and me. "Come here, I want to take our picture."

Grabbing my hand, he pulls me toward the full-length mirror. He wraps his arm around my waist, and I do the same. I prepare to smile at the mirror, but he tells me to kiss him instead. That's exactly what I do.

"Let me see."

Jett hands me his phone and I smile at our picture. We're the perfect height difference and we just fit together.

"Send it to me."

He presses a few buttons and smiles at me. "What do you say we go out tonight?" With quick moves, he twirls me around. "We could dance and have some drinks."

That does sound fun, but will he be recognized? Are they going to take picture after picture? I know this is one side of his fame that I suppose I'll need to get used to if I want to be with him. "That sounds fun."

"Good, let's take a nap, and then we'll eat a late dinner." Jett picks me up and tosses me onto the bed.

I laugh as I bounce a couple of times before coming to a stop. Patting the spot next to me, he dives onto the bed. We snuggle chest to chest and our legs tangled together. "You're not getting tired of me, are you?" Yikes, I can't believe I just asked that.

"Never, not even a little. You've made this so much more fun." Jett kisses me softly.

We snuggle close and then take the best fucking nap.

The bouncer at Paradise nightclub speaks into a little headset as Jett and I stand next to the velvet rope. A few minutes later, a man in a nice-looking black suit comes out and his smile is big and wide as he approaches us.

"Mr. Hamilton, welcome to Paradise."

We follow him inside. Jett decided to not do anything to disguise himself. If he did, it would just draw more attention to him. He leads us to a table that sits on an elevated platform. A woman comes toward us with a bucket of champagne and two glasses.

"This is on the house. Please let us know if you need anything else," the man says before they leave us.

Jett pours each of us a glass. "To you, gorgeous," he says as he holds his glass out.

I do the same and we clink them together. "And to you. This place is so cool." If heaven was a bar, it would look like this. It is all white tea light-looking lights. White draperies are everywhere and even the seats and tables are white. There is some fresh greenery that fills in the empty spaces.

The music is great, and the dance floor is filled with people. I've always loved dancing and *I think* I'm pretty good at it.

"It is. Xavier has been here before and I texted him earlier, asking where I could take you," Jett says as he places his hand on my thigh.

I'm wearing the halter dress and sandals that I got here. I put my hair in a bubble ponytail and did my makeup to give me a dewy glow. He's in jeans and a tight T-shirt that shows off his lean, muscled body. His light brown hair is slicked back, and his face is covered in a little bit of stubble.

It takes no time before we finish the bottle. He orders himself a vodka soda and I order a spicy margarita. The server brings our drinks and I don't like the way she leans in toward Jett, but he doesn't even pay her any attention. I, on the other hand, look up at her.

"That'll be all, thanks."

She gives me a snooty look, but then leaves us. I sit back and feel mortified about the way I just behaved. All I want to do is run, but Jett just pulls me into his side, kissing me deeply. He pulls away and I'm in such a kiss fog that I sway toward him. His chuckle is deep and makes goose bumps pop up all over my skin.

While we drink and I dance in my seat, Jett swallows down the rest of his drink and stands up. Holding his hand out to me, he smiles.

"Let's dance, baby."

He doesn't have to ask me twice. I take his hand and he leads me to the dance floor. We move to the beat of the music, my arms wrapped around his shoulders. There isn't an inch of space between us as we grind together like we're fucking.

I can feel eyes on us, but I'm buzzed just enough not to care. Jett's hands slide down my back and settle just above my ass. Song after song, we move to the music, and it is evident that he's a good dancer.

His eyes hold mine, and even under the strobe lights, I can feel the intensity of them. Even though there are people watching, he kisses me again, and I melt into him. I'm addicted to his kisses, and it isn't long before I'm sinking into them.

I have to go to the bathroom. "I'll be right back." With a hand to the small of my back, he leads me back up the stairs. He sits down at our table and I head toward the restroom. In the VIP section, there's its own set of bathrooms.

Inside the bathroom, it's totally bougee, but I love it. There is one woman waiting ahead of me so while I wait, I get on my phone. There's a text from Miles.

**Miles:** Hey, baby sister. Just checking in. Also, I wanted to remind you that at the end of the week, I'm heading to New York for that signing and proposing to Victoria. Mona just sent out a group text, you and the actor look cozy. Be careful and if he hurts you, I'll kill him.

Smiling, I shake my head. Always the protector, that's my brother for you. I open the attachment he sent and see that it's a picture from tonight. It is Jett and I kissing on the dance floor. God, this makes me feel icky.

I mean, yeah, this is a great picture, but someone took our picture and posted it without our permission.

Instead of responding to that, I wish him luck with his proposal.

| | |
|---|---|
| **Greta:** | I'm so happy for you both, and I hope it all goes well. If he hurts me, I'll let you 	 Just kidding. Love you big brother, and again pre-congratulations. |

I stick my phone back in my bag, and luckily, it's my turn. After I finish up, I wash my hands and look at myself in the mirror. I look really, really happy, and that scares me. I'm unsure if this is just a fling or something more. My heart is already totally invested in this, whatever it is.

Heading back out, I find Jett with two women taking a selfie with him. He's smiling with his hands resting on the table. An arm grabs my bicep roughly. I let a squeak out as I'm jerked back into a hard chest.

I jerk away from them and turn. He goes to grab me again, but I step back. "Hey, I want to dance with you."

"No, sorry, I'm with someone." I walk backward and run into another hard body, but thankfully I know this one.

Jett steadies me with his hands and then moves me to the side. That's when I feel the angry vibe coming off him. "You got a problem, mate?" He starts moving toward him. "Did you touch her?" He gets closer and I get between them. "Move, Greta." His voice is low and pissed. It's a side of him I haven't seen and I don't like it.

"Baby, please. Let's go back to the house." I look deep into his eyes. "Please."

# eighteen

## JETT

"Please," Greta says softly, pleading with her eyes. She somehow breaks through my anger, and I back away from him. "Let's leave, please."

I nod and grab her hand. We move around the fucking asshole who had the nerve to touch her. I've never in my life felt jealousy like I did when I watched him grab her. The look on her face pissed me off even more. He scared her and all I saw was red.

Our driver picks us up and takes us back to the house. I help her out and lead her inside. No one else is here, so we have the house to ourselves. I pin her to the wall next to the door.

"The minute he put his hands on you, I swear I wanted to rip his fucking head off."

I nip at her lower lip. "No one has ever been able to calm me when I've been on the edge.

Especially with as fast as I could feel myself escalating. Thank you." I kiss her, easing her mouth open with my lips. Brushing my tongue against hers, her unique flavor explodes on my tongue.

She pulls her mouth from mine. "I could tell you were mad. I could feel it. I knew people were watching us, and I didn't want you doing something that could have people talking bad about you."

Why do I really, really like that she's looking out for me? That she's trying to protect my image. Except for family, Josiah, Kim, and a few others, I don't trust many people to have my back. It feels good knowing that I've got Greta too.

I kiss her one more time before grabbing her hand and dragging her out to the pool. The pool is private, meaning that no one can see it unless they're here.

"What are we doing?" she asks, sitting on the lounger.

Instead of answering her, I grab the hem of my shirt and pull it over my head. Greta watches me with hungry eyes as I strip off my pants, leaving me in a pair of boxer briefs. She does the same except she's just in a pair of white lace panties.

I take a quick second to enjoy the view. Fuck, she's perfection... every inch of her. Her breasts are firm and perky with hoops I love to tug on. My dick is hard, and I don't even try to hide it as I take her hand and lead her into the pool.

We swim around, making out in between. She wraps around me like a spider monkey as we float in the middle of the pool.

"What happens when we go back to America?" Greta's voice is quiet as she asks.

"I want to be honest with you, I don't know."

She may want nothing to do with me once she finds out the truth, but I'm not ready to tell her yet. Especially now that I've developed real feelings for her. I didn't want to like her more than just someone to hang out with and be there to make me look good, but in no time, I did.

"Okay," she says quietly. Greta lays her head on my shoulder and hugs me close.

I hate that she seems disappointed, but the last thing I wanted to do was lead her on. It would only hurt her. Hugging her, I kick my feet to keep us above the water.

She kisses me and then pulls away. "I'm going to go to bed."

I watch her climb out of the pool, scoop up her clothes, and then disappear inside. "Fuck, fuck, fuck." Muttering, I swim toward the steps and climb out.

Inside, I give her a little alone time. I pull a beer out of the fridge and crack it open. Chugging it down, I let out a loud belch before locking the house. Upstairs I step into the bedroom and find Greta in bed, asleep. I quickly dry off and then slide in beside her. She thankfully rolls toward me and wraps her arm around my waist.

"I'm sorry I reacted badly," she says softly. "Of course, you don't know. We haven't been... whatever this is for very long."

She settles in under my chin and promptly passes out. It is a long time before I fall asleep because I know I need to tell her the truth and then we'll be able to talk about what happens next.

I sit across the pool, watching Greta read the script for *Vague Shadows*. Josiah brought it yesterday, and she had asked to read it. Luckily, things have been fine between us. She's been affectionate and her usually funny self, thank fuck.

Drinking coffee, I thumb through my phone. I google Greta and me, and I smile. There are lots of pictures of us. People are again, speculating if she's the one, and my eyes drift to her. She's got tears running down her cheeks.

I grab my coffee and walk around the pool and lay down on the lounger next to her. Watching her while I drink my coffee, I'm dying to know what she thinks. She pays me no mind while she continues to flip the pages of the script.

Setting my cup down, I get into the pool. I swim laps over and over until my arms feel like Jell-O. Greta is sitting up when I get out. "What'd you think?" sitting down across from her, I ask.

She holds it up into the air. "This is possibly the most beautiful piece of writing I've ever read," she says excitedly as she gets up on her knees, hugging the pages to her chest. "I love it so much. Grayson is so damaged, and he just wants to do right by his little brother."

The conviction in her tone makes me smile. "I only got to read a summary of the story, but I know I want it."

Greta gets off her lounger and pushes me back on mine. She climbs on top of me, straddling me, and shaking the script in my face. "You are totally Grayson." She sets the script down before leaning down. "Let me hear your American accent."

"Ahem... you want to hear my American accent, huh?"

Greta claps and then leans down, kissing my lips.

"I take it, you like it?" I worked with a coach to perfect my accents.

She nods. "It's great and sounds really natural."

"What kind of guy do you think Grayson is?" I ask her with my hands on her hips.

Greta pushes up and bites her lip. Fuck me, she's a vision. "I think at the beginning, he's just kind of drifting through life. He's got a job that pays well, but it's not his dream job. All of his relationships have been unfulfilling. When his mom dies, and he gets custody of his brother, everything changes for him. In the end, he finds his purpose." Her cheeks turn pink and she turns away from me. "Ugh, sorry that was so nerdy."

"Not at all. Thank you for reading it." I brush her hair out of her face. "I've never wanted a role more."

"Well, I hope you get it."

Pulling her down, I kiss her slowly. Fuck, I can't stop kissing her. "I'm addicted to your lips."

"Awww... aren't you the sweetest." He flashes us a smile that looks forced. "Ahem... sorry to interrupt." Josiah says with a laugh.

I freeze and find him sitting on the lounger one over from us. That doesn't sit real well with me, but now's not the time to talk to him about it. I quickly lift Greta off me and keep her right next to me when I sit up.

"What's going on?"

"Nothing. Just wanted to check in before I head back to LA. I'm going to meet with Kim about the shooting schedule for the movie. I want to be prepared for when you get it." He winks at Greta and I don't miss the way she leans in closer to me. I'm thinking she doesn't like him. I may have to dig deeper into that.

I stand up, hoping he takes the hint and leaves. Thankfully he does and follows us into the house. "Sounds good. I appreciate you getting the script here." We share a half handshake, backslapping hug. "Thanks for everything."

"Of course. I'll get someone to open your house, get it cleaned up, and get some groceries for you before you get back." Josiah walks toward the door.

I turn to Greta. "I'm gonna walk him out. I'll be right back."

She pushes up on her toes and kisses my lips. "Okay, I'm going to go lay down. I stayed up too late reading." Attempting to wink at me, it looks more like a twitch, which makes me laugh. "Now, get out of here." Greta waves to Josiah as she walks by. "Have a safe flight."

Outside, Josiah stops next to his rental. "I didn't expect you to be all touchy-feely with her when you're behind closed doors. Are you starting to like her? Is this becoming real?"

"What do you mean?" I'm not going to admit to him that I do like her or that I'm falling deeply for her. "This is, what it is."

He steps in close to me. "You need to watch yourself. She's a distraction you don't need."

I'm shocked he said that because that's the furthest from the truth. Sure, I love being around her, but she's not a distraction. "Don't worry, I promise you my eye is on the prize."

Josiah nods and then climbs into his rental. I stand outside until his car disappears. Taking a moment, wondering what the fuck I am going to do.

Inside, I head upstairs and look in on Greta. Her soft snores greet me when I step into the room, making me smile. Back downstairs, I grab my phone and see a text from Bruno.

> **Bruno:** Hey man, I heard you're one of the actors they're auditioning for that new film everyone is talking about. Congrats, brother.

I quickly type out my response.

> **Jett:** Thanks, mate. I'm thrilled.

> **Bruno:** You should be. Hey, tell Greta I finished her brother's book and I'll send it to her.

We make plans to get together when I get back to LA, and I ignore the fact that he's asked me about bringing Greta. I decide to head downstairs to the gym. Hopping on the treadmill, I run until I'm exhausted. Covered in sweat, I head upstairs and hop in the shower.

After washing up, I head back into our bedroom. She stirs as I get dressed, and I climb onto the bed with her.

"Did you have a good nap?"

She stretches and then smiles. "I did. Everything okay with Josiah?"

"Oh yeah. We just had some stuff to go over when I go back to LA."

Her smile falls, but she quickly hides it. "What's the plan for today?" Greta wraps her arms around me, pulling me down to the bed.

"I just thought we could walk around for a while. Just go exploring." I kiss her. "How does that sound?"

Greta's smile is wide and bright, and it makes my heart squeeze. "That sounds like so much fun. I just need to freshen up." She shoves me off her and disappears into the bathroom. Her giggle can be heard through the door.

God, she is something else.

# nineteen

## GRETA

Sitting up in bed, I reach over and touch Jett's side of the bed. It is still slightly warm. He must've just gotten up. I throw on a tank top and cotton shorts before heading in search of my man.

After a quick search, I find a note on the counter that just says "jogging." It makes me laugh and I pick it up. Folding it up, I stick it into my wallet. Just something to remember him by. Gosh, why does that hurt to think about it?

He's made no promises and maybe I was naïve to think that this was going to become something more. That's on me though, and not on Jett. Will any other man be enough, or will my expectations be too outrageously high?

Oh god, am I a mess or what? I grab my phone and decide to check my social media and to see what's being said about me.

I scroll through the headlines and freeze. *Jett Hamilton in "fake" relationship?*

"What?"

I open the article. "A source close to the actor says that the relationship with Greta Collins is all a charade. The source says that she's clueless and had no clue that the relationship wasn't real."

My eyes burn and my stomach turns. Especially after I check other sites and find the same thing. I bolt for the bathroom, emptying the contents of my stomach into the toilet. After rinsing my mouth out and brushing my teeth, I head downstairs, waiting for Jett to get back.

The sound of the front door opening causes me to start bouncing my leg up and down. My hands begin to tremble, and my eyes burn again, but I blink the feeling away. He steps into the living room and stops when he sees me.

"Good morning, beautiful. Did you just get up?" He walks toward me, but when I look up at him, he stops. "Hey, are you okay?"

I shake my head. "Were you just pretending to be into me? Was this all an act?"

Jett stiffens. "I can explain," he says quietly.

That is when the tears can no longer be blinked away begin to roll down my cheeks. "Explain? Explain what? You used me, you made me feel like you cared about me. So, what was the purpose? What did you have to gain from humiliating me?" I stand up, crossing my arms. "Tell me, I have a right to know." I shout.

He shakes his head. "I-I first want to say that I wouldn't have gone along with this if I hadn't enjoyed hanging out with you." Jett starts to walk toward me, but I back away. He takes the hint and stops. "You know I've had a reputation, and I'll admit most of it is true, but a lot is just tabloid fodder. Josiah suggested I spend time with someone and make it look like we're in a relationship. That would show them that I was taking things seriously."

"Oh my god. I was a prop, and you don't care about me at all, do you?" I ball my fists into a ball, and cry it this time. "Do you?"

He doesn't say anything, and I know that it's true. My heart shatters and I run for the stairs, tripping on my way up, but I don't care. Up in our room, I grab my bag out of the closet and grab the few clothes I have, shoving them into it.

In the bathroom, I grab my toiletries and throw them into the bag. I take a second to take a deep breath. I grab some tissues to dry the tears spilling from my eyes. Fuck, what do I do? I'm in a different country.

Grabbing my bag, I head back into the bedroom. I was half expecting him to be here, trying to talk to me, but instead I've got an empty room. I've got no clue where I'm going, but I need to go somewhere because I can't stay here with him.

I walk down the stairs and find Jett sitting on the sofa. He stands when I come down. "Greta, please. Let's talk about this. Let me explain."

"Explain what? You used me, you played with my emotions," I cry. God, I don't want him seeing me like this. At the door, I turn to look at him. "This really fucking sucks, and to think I realized I was falling in love with you last night before I fell asleep."

I step outside and start walking and have no clue where I'm going. Ten minutes or more later, I end up in front of a market and step inside. At the counter, I step up to the woman behind it. "Hi, do you speak English?"

"Yes, I do. May I help?" She looks to be my mom's age. She's beautiful with her long dark brown waves.

Pasting a fake smile on, I look the woman in the eye. "I was wondering if there is a hotel nearby. Umm... my accommodations fell through, and I am looking for a place to stay just until I can fly home tomorrow." I know I'm babbling, but I'm very close to breaking down again.

She comes around the counter, looping her arm through mine. "There's a lovely hotel at the end of the street. My daughter is actually the manager there." We head to the door. "I'll walk you down there." The woman tells a teenager at the end of an aisle something in Greek. She then turns back to me.

"Thank you. I appreciate it." I suck in a breath and walk beside her until we reach a beautiful driveway lined with flowers. "This is beautiful," I tell her.

"*Vai*. Yes, it is. My name is Rhea," she tells me as we reach the door.

I smile and nod. "Nice to meet you, Rhea. I'm Greta."

We step inside the reception area, and I follow her to the counter. She speaks Greek to the woman behind the desk, and then she gets up and disappears through a door. When she returns, she's followed by a woman who looks to be my age. She smiles at Rhea and comes around the counter to hug her.

They speak back and forth, I'm only able to pick out my name. "Hi, I'm Athena. My mother says you need a room for the night?"

I take her hand, shaking it. "Nice meeting you, and yes, I just need a room while I work on travel arrangements. I hope to be leaving tomorrow."

"I do have a couple of rooms. I have one with a balcony view or just a very basic room that's in the semi-basement," she tells me.

If it is clean, I don't care where I sleep. "The basic room is fine. I don't want to take the room with a view from someone who will enjoy it."

Rhea leaves us and I pay for my room. Shit, my savings account is going to take a hit, but whatever, I'll work extra hard when I get home. Athena shows me to my room, and it is super cute. I turn to look at her. "Thank you so much. This is great."

Thankfully she leaves me be. I climb on the bed and begin to sob again. My heart aches and I'm so hurt. He used me, and everyone knows. I'm a laughingstock, a clueless idiot who fell for an actor.

Grabbing my phone, I quickly block Jett. Of course, I don't know why I did, he didn't even try to stop me from leaving. Great, now I'm crying harder. I dial my brother. I know he's in New York, but he's the one I need.

"Hey, everything okay?" His voice low and scratchy from sleep.

"Miles?" I wipe the tears that spill from my eyes. "Miles, I want to come home." I start sobbing. Fuck, why does it hurt so much?

"Greta, what's going on?" His voice breaks through my tears.

"I-I don't want to talk about it. Please come get me." I don't recognize my own voice right now. "I'm in Greece."

I hear rustling around. "Okay, sweetheart. Victoria and I are in New York. Let me make some arrangements, and we'll get you home; I promise."

I cry harder.

"Gret, are you going to be okay? We're going to come to you."

I grab a tissue and blow my nose. "I'll be okay until you get here. I'll text you where I'm at."

"Okay, good. Try to get some sleep, and I'll text you when we get on the plane and text you when we land." I hug the pillow to my chest when he speaks again. "You are going to get through this, okay? I love you."

"I love you too, Miles. Thank you for coming to get me."

Stepping off the plane in Paris, I head outside to catch a cab to take to the private airfield I'm meeting Miles and Victoria at. Yesterday they had called me and were flying me to Paris where I'd meet them, and we'd take Victoria's dad's plane home.

All I did last night was cry, eat, and sleep. The story about Jett and me exploded everywhere, and people wanted to know more about our whole fake relationship.

A cab pulls up and I hand him the address for the airfield. Luckily, it's not that far to the airport. They arrived late last night, and I feel terrible that they're going to be turning right back around and flying home.

Of course, they wouldn't be doing it if they didn't want to. I've kept my sunglasses on since I left the hotel in Santorini. My eyes are puffy and bloodshot, and my bags have bags. I'm mentally and emotionally exhausted.

He pulls up in front of the airplane hangar, and I spot Miles talking to a man in a uniform. I pay the driver and grab my bag before climbing out. My brother spots me and makes his way to me. The minute I'm in his arms, I'm sobbing again.

I think he is talking to me, but I can't be sure as he leads me toward the plane and Victoria comes around the corner. Stepping away from my brother, I hug her tightly.

"Come on, sweetheart." She leads me onto the plane, and the other woman gets me situated in a seat.

Victoria hands me a glass with caramel-colored liquid. "Drink this, sweetheart."

I do as she says, finishing the drink in two swallows. The warmth slides down my throat and into my belly. Neither of them asks me for more details about what happened, which I'm grateful for. Miles puts a plate in front of me that's filled with pastries and fruit.

Munching on a croissant, I stare out the window as we take off. I watch as Paris gets smaller and smaller. God, we're heading home. This is all over. I grab my phone, and because I'm a glutton for punishment, I open the photo app and thumb through the pictures of Jett and me.

My favorite picture is from the other night. We were snuggling on the lounger together. Our pictures definitely showed how good we looked together. Great, the tears begin to fall again.

Victoria wraps her arms around me, and I cry myself to sleep with my head on her shoulder.

# twenty

## JETT

Letting myself into my house, I drop my bags by the door. On autopilot, I head into the kitchen, grab the bottle of tequila, pull the cork out, and take a couple of deep pulls. I set it down and head back to my bedroom.

I strip off my clothes and step into the shower. Standing under the spray, I let it rinse the grime from traveling off my body. Fuck, I can't stop seeing the look on Greta's face before she left. She was so fucking hurt and when she told me she was falling in love with me, I felt like I had been punched in the gut.

My first mistake was not going after her, but I'm in uncharted territory here. I've never had a relationship and in my fucked-up head, I was just giving her some time, but then she wouldn't answer my calls or texts and I couldn't find her.

I made the mistake of getting online and googling us. "Fuck," I mutter. Every article I read is talking shit about us, especially me.

Josiah called an hour ago to tell me that he was releasing a statement on my behalf. He was going to investigate who leaked the story. Whoever did is going to fucking pay, that's for fucking sure.

God, I miss her already. That wasn't supposed to happen, and I wasn't supposed to have feelings for her, but dammit, I did. I miss her smile, her melodic laugh, and her gorgeous body. I have never connected to another woman before, especially one I was sleeping with.

After climbing out of the shower, I wrap my towel around my waist and step into my room. I shut the room darkening shades and collapse onto the bed. I'm exhausted but every time I close my eyes, I see the look on her face.

This is for the best though—long-distance relationships don't work, especially in this industry. Greta will realize this was for the best.

I need to stop, it's becoming an addiction, but one I welcome. A week ago, Greta started posting on social media again and ever since, I've been stalking her online. She posted a picture the other day of her with her nieces and nephew, and I could see that her smile didn't reach her eyes.

It didn't take long to realize that she blocked me because I've tried to call and text her, and I can't get through and texts go unread. I'm so far out of my depth here. Josiah is coming over to get me caught up on anything I missed while I was gone. He swears he doesn't know how the story was leaked, and honestly, I'm not sure if I believe him or not.

I've got a meeting later with someone who can find out for me. Until then, I'm not going to do anything. If he did leak it, he's fucked, but I want to have proof first. What would he have to gain by leaking it? The whole point of everything with Greta was supposed to improve my image.

Shit, that sounds bad, but that *was* the original plan. I head into my home gym, turn on Rage Against the Machine, and begin jumping rope.

After two hours, I am finally finished. I shower and then shave before throwing on a pair of board shorts. In the kitchen, I make myself some scrambled eggs loaded with veggies. Sitting at the counter, I pull up Instagram and watch Greta's newest video like a fucking creep.

I notice that her cheek piercings are gone, as well as her septum. She does have a new rose gold hoop in her nose. She looks beautiful with or without the piercings. Her hair is still lightened from the sun and her skin is still beautifully tan.

The comment section is shut off, and I wonder why. Were people starting to fuck with her because of me in the comments? Goddamn, this fucking sucks. I want to be with her right now and making sure she's okay.

I exit out of the app before I obsess about her anymore for the day. Keys in the door alert me to Josiah's arrival. Sticking my plate in the sink, I take a deep breath, praying for the strength not to throttle him, at least not yet.

"How's it going?" Josiah says as he steps around the corner. He sets his laptop on the breakfast bar before making himself an espresso. "Are you back on your regular sleeping schedule?"

"Pretty much, mate. The house looked great when I got home. Thanks for that." I lean against the granite countertop. "I'm starting to work on my audition piece. It's a great story, and I'm totally Grayson."

"It's a great script. If you get the role, or I should say *when* you get it. You'll be off to Georgia to film."

Georgia, Greta lives in Atlanta. God, that would be perfect, but I can't wait until then. I need to figure out how to fix things. I want something real with her, something that I can feel is going to turn into something important. I turn to Josiah.

"That sounds really good, mate. Anything else going on that I should know about?"

He sips his espresso. "You're going to need to do some ADR for *Summer Heat,* and I'm just waiting to find out for sure when they'll need you at the studio. I heard from George, and he'll have the proofs from the photoshoot soon."

"Cool, thanks. I appreciate it."

I load my dishwasher while he types away on his laptop. My mum would kick my ass if I wasn't cleaning up after myself. He wouldn't suspect anything since it isn't unusual for us to be silent while we're together. Josiah is always working on something. He looks up from his laptop.

"You doing okay? You seem off."

Of course, I'm off. The girl that I fell for was hurt and is hurting because of me. Because Josiah gave me shitty advice and more than likely leaked our story to the media. She deserves better than me, but

I'm still going to go to her and fight for us.

For once in my life, I'm going to put in the maximum effort for a woman. We'll figure out the distance thing, we can make it work.

I nod. "Yeah, man, I'm good. Still a little jet laggy, but it's getting better."

He must buy it because he nods and closes his laptop. "Good, and be ready because I just got an email from the casting agent, and she'd like you to come in to read next week. They plan on narrowing it down to two of you, and then you'll do a test screening with Justin Moore, who will play the brother. They'll make their decision after that."

"I'll be ready." Fuck, this means winning back Greta will have to wait just a little bit longer.

After he leaves, I grab my keys and head into my garage, climbing into my Audi. It takes me an hour to reach downtown LA. This guy I'm meeting was recommended by my lawyer. Thankfully he didn't ask any questions about why I needed to meet this guy. He just let me know that he was there if I needed him for anything legal.

I find a parking spot two blocks away from the bar I'm meeting Hank. Once I reach Dice, I pull my hat down a little farther to hopefully cover my face a little more. Scanning the bar, I spot who I'm guessing is him, sitting in the corner booth, facing the door.

"Hank," I say as I reach the table.

He stands up. "Jett?"

I nod.

"Good meeting you. Let's sit."

"You came highly recommended by Vince. I appreciate you coming." The bartender stops at our booth, and we order a couple of beers. "Did he tell you what I wanted?"

He nods. "Yeah. You think your manager leaked the story about you and your girlfriend."

The title girlfriend isn't freaking me out. I kind of like it, which fucking sucks because she's not here, and I wish she was. *Okay focus*, I tell myself.

"Unless he told someone, he's the only one who knew about it. Who else would do it?"

"It does sound like it. I'll make some calls and ask some questions. Keeping it anonymous, of course. I have my ways to get information and will keep you updated."

The bartender drops off our beers.

He left after he finished his beer, and I hung out for one more.

I then head home to read the script, practice my monologue, and figure out a way to get Greta back.

# twenty one

## GRETA

I blink away the sleep and throw back the covers. God, my body feels heavy as I climb out of bed. When will I get over him? I've been home for two weeks, and I've finally stopped crying myself to sleep, but I still have photographers following me. Twice we've had to lock the doors at the studio due to reporters coming in and wanting to interview me.

Joaquin hired a security guard and now only people with appointments are allowed in. Even my piercing customers have to have appointments. Luckily everyone has been great and understanding. I hate feeling like I'm some sort of spectacle.

My sisters, their partners, my brother and his fiancée

have all been so supportive. Right now, I'm staying with Miles and Victoria because I can't be alone right now. I didn't want to stay with them since they just got engaged, but they insisted. At least their apartment is big enough that I don't feel like I'm in their way.

Mom called last night, checking in. She wanted me to come down to Arizona for a week or two, but I told her I couldn't keep hiding. The photographers and reporters will eventually stop bothering me. They'll find another story and I'll be back to my normal life, maybe.

I take a quick shower and then throw on some black leggings and one of my Imagine Dragons concert T-shirts. In the kitchen, I find my brother and future sister-in-law talking quietly together while drinking coffee.

"Good morning," I say as I take the coffee that Victoria pours for me. "Thanks."

Miles wraps his arm around me and gives me a squeeze. "How did you sleep last night?"

I know my brother is worried, but that's because they were the ones who saw what a mess I was when they flew to Paris to get me.

"Okay, I just wish I could just get over him and move on." I take a sip of my coffee and sigh. "I'm just exhausted."

"I've got to head to my office, but just come get me if you need me." Miles kisses Victoria and I smile. They're so perfect together. He passes by me and kisses the top of my head before he disappears into their bedroom with his laptop.

Victoria steps toward me and asks quietly. "Are you okay... for real? No bullshit."

My eyes burn and I shake my head. "Why do I still feel something for him? We knew each other for only a few weeks. It does not happen that fast."

"I fell for your brother the moment I met him. Look at your sisters too. They all fell fast and hard. You can't help how you feel." She rubs my arm. "No one can tell you it is too soon."

Pulling her into a hug, I squeeze her tight. "I'll never be able to thank you for everything."

"We're family. That's what we do."

I kiss her cheek and then take my coffee to my room. After doing my makeup, I slip on my socks and shoes, grab my phone, and stick it in my purse. The studio doesn't open until ten unless one of the girls schedules a client early. I'm going in early for that hour of alone time. I'll just turn on some tunes while I stock everyone's stations.

It takes me twenty minutes to get to the studio, and once I let myself inside, I relock the door and flip on the light. Behind the front desk, I plug in my phone and turn on my favorite playlist. In the stockroom, I load it with the stuff each sister and Laney likes.

I get everything unloaded and organized. Then I polish all the chrome, mop the floor, and clean my piercing room. I'm doing a Prince Albert today and I get everything out that I need. After grabbing my phone, I head down the hall and let myself into the office. Flopping down on the love seat, I kick my feet up on the coffee table.

Looking at my phone, I decide to torture myself and look at pictures of us. One of my favorites is us lying in bed. I had my head on his shoulder and his lips were on my forehead. Tears well up in my eyes.

That was a good morning. We had laid in bed just talking, napping, and making out. I wipe the tear that slides down my cheek.

I'm fucking stupid, that's what I am. I get on my social media and see a lot of people have slid into my DMs. It sucks that most of the messages are people asking about Jett and usually they're mean. Unfortunately, I have to weed through them to get to the legitimate messages.

I respond to the ones that are fans of mine and have been for a while. Against my better judgment, I pull up Jett and see if there is anything posted by him. Is he already hooking up with other women?

There doesn't seem to be any evidence that he is. Ugh... what is wrong with me. I close the app and set my phone down on the coffee table. I lean back on the love seat and close my eyes. Soon we'll be open, and we can get this day started and just maybe, I'll be a little bit closer to getting over him.

I park my car and climb out. Reaching into the passenger side, I grab the cup carrier. Carrying the coffees inside. I set them down on the counter.

"Coffee break," I call out.

Mona comes out from the back office.

"I just love that color." My sister changes her hair color a lot but each time it is gorgeous. It's a smoky gray right now, but damn, it suits her.

"Oh my god, thank you for grabbing these. I was up late making treats for the kids' school bake sale." She takes a sip and exaggerates a sigh. "Mmmm... that is so good."

"You're such a good mom," I tell her.

My niece and nephew are both eight years old. Max belongs to Mona's fiancé, and we all adopted him.

She smiles at me. "They're easy kids. How are you?"

I shrug and shake my head. "Taking it day by day, and that's about all I can do." Kissing her cheek, I grab the other girls their drinks and pass them out.

Heidi is working on a piece, so I set her tea on her counter. My sister just told me that she and Colton are having a baby, and his cancer is back. I hate that they're going through this—she's so strong and they will get through this, and they know they have all of us to help them.

I don't want to interrupt her while she works, so I move on and hand Lainey her drink. "Is this a piece you're working on today?" Looking down at the drawing she's working on.

"It is. What do you think?" It's a stack of books with pages spilling out and floating around them.

"Gorgeous. I can't wait to see it when it's all finished." I hand her, her cup, and then head back to the front desk. Taking a sip of my coffee, I pull up the girls' schedules and set up the text reminders for their appointments. After sending them, I straighten up the waiting area.

The door opens and I turn to greet whoever just walked in. I freeze and then smile tentatively as Bruno Nixon himself steps inside and flashes me that big white smile.

"Hey, sweetheart."

Without a second thought, I step right into his open arms. I return his hug and then step back. "Hi! It is so good to see you. What are you doing here? Not that it isn't nice to see you." Ugh... I am such a dork.

He throws his arm around my shoulders. "I'm here for two reasons. First, I'm actually meeting your brother here. Secondly, I wanted to see how you were doing?"

I look up at him and wonder if he's here asking for himself or if Jett wanted to know. Who am I kidding? He doesn't care about me, he never did. Shit. *Blink, blink, blink.* I stop the burning in my eyes. "Ahem... I'm okay. I'm not used to all the attention."

We sit on the sofa in the waiting area. "He's miserable," Bruno says. "And he fired Josiah."

My eyes widen. "What? Why?"

"He's the one who leaked the story, and that's all I can really tell you. Jett fucked up, and he knows it."

The door opens and my brother steps inside. "Hey, big brother." I'm thankful for the interruption. I stand up and hug him. "Come officially meet Bruno."

They shake hands, and then Bruno winks at me as he walks by and then outside with Miles. God, that was so weird. Did a famous actor just come into our studio? Did the man just hug me and then leave with my brother?

"Ummm... who the heck was that?" Sierra says from behind me with Ember in her arms.

I grab my niece and snuggle her close. She and her cousins are a natural antidepressant for me. Breathing in my niece's sweet baby powder scent, I sigh. I don't feel as sad as I felt earlier. She grabs my hair in her tiny little fist.

"No, no, no, sweet girl." I look at her mommy. "That was Bruno Nixon."

"What? Are you serious? Did I see him and Miles leave together?" She runs to the window, looking out like a crazy stalker, making me laugh.

"You did. I'm not sure what they're doing together, but I'm sure if there is something we should know, Miles will tell us."

Ember starts fussing, so I start lightly bouncing up and down. Thankfully, she begins to settle.

Sierra comes back to me. "He's a friend of Jett's, right?"

I nod. "Yeah, I met him in California. He's really nice." Ember starts to cry, and I hand her to her mom. "She's changed so much already." It's amazing how she's developing this little personality.

"I'm going to go nurse her, but we need to talk soon." She carries her daughter down the hall and closes the office door.

I get behind the desk and answer the phone.

# twenty two

## JETT

My flight lands in Atlanta, and I have no idea what the fuck I'm doing, and I've got no plan. All I know is that my life has turned upside down since I met Greta. Earlier this week, I fired Josiah. I knew he was the one who leaked the story, but when he told me why, it took all the restraint I had to not throttle him.

He said he'd been watching us in Greece and could see I was falling for her. The asshole thought she'd become a distraction and then he wouldn't make as much money from me. I told him if I ever heard from him again that I would sue him for defamation of character.

Luckily Bruno's manager is going to help me out until I find a new one. Speaking of my friend, he's already in Atlanta meeting with Greta's brother. I tried to pry information out of him, but he wouldn't say anything.

Yesterday was my audition, and the monologue I chose was emotional and to feel the emotion I needed for Grayson, I pictured the look on Greta's face when she told me she was falling in love with me.

Needless to say, I nailed that fucking audition. I'm not sure when I'll hear, but the minute I could leave LA, I was on the first flight here. They turn the seat belt sign off and I stand up, grabbing my backpack. First class is let off the plane first, and I make my way off the tarmac.

Security is waiting at the gate for me to escort me through the airport. I don't stop for people, I'm just too anxious to get to Greta. I do smile and wave but keep walking. I don't know why I bothered wearing a baseball cap and sunglasses, I'm not fooling anyone.

Outside, I climb into the back of the black Navigator. Due to traffic, it takes a half hour to get to the Four Seasons. Once inside, the manager shows me up to my suite. I tip him and take the key card.

Tossing my backpack on the sofa, I pull out the one change of clothes I brought and toss them on the bed in the bedroom. Stripping out of my clothes, I climb into the shower. After a quick scrub down, I hop out and throw on my boxer briefs.

My phone rings and I see it's my mum. "Hey."

I'm unsure how this talk is going to go. She's pissed at me, which unfortunately has happened a lot over the years. As soon as the hormones kicked in, I became a nightmare.

"Hi honey. I've decided I'm done being mad. Your father says you're in Atlanta. Are you going to make things right with Greta?" My mum stalked her on social media and is team Greta.

"I'm going to try. I don't know what I'm doing." I'm going to screw this up, I know it, but I'll regret it if I don't.

Mum sighs. "Sweetheart, just be honest about how you feel and why you did what you did. You messed up and hurt her. If you really want to be with her and see where this goes, then don't give up."

Before hanging up, I promise to call her with an update when I have one. After getting dressed, I text Bruno, asking him where he's at. He knows I'm here, and he's going to be with Greta's family.

He's been talking to Miles and making a case for me, at least to get me an invite. If I just show up, I'm not sure it would be welcomed. While I wait, I sit on the sofa and start flipping through the channels.

The driver pulls into the driveway of a large white home that looks like a cottage. There are several other cars in the driveway, and I start to get a little nervous. I swear that's never happened to me before. Climbing out of the SUV, I ask the driver to hang out until I'm ready and walk toward the front door.

# GRETA

My heart races and butterflies take flight in my belly as I watch Jett walk toward me. He smiles softly as he reaches me.

"Hi," I say lamely. "Sorry about your face."

He moves his sore jaw back and forth. "Your brother is fast."

I laugh softly but then remind myself what he did and cross my arms over my chest. "What are you doing here?" I try not to look directly at him. He's so beautiful, and I don't want it clouding my judgment. "Actually, I don't care why you're here. What you did to me was so humiliating. You used me to help you get a movie role."

"I know. What I did was a terrible lapse in judgment. I wanted to tell you the plan, but Josiah said we could sell it better if you believed it." He scrubs his hands over his face. "It sounds terrible, I know this. You were someone I liked hanging out with, and we had a lot of chemistry. It was going to be no hardship hanging out with you. I knew I needed to tell you the whole time, but I was afraid that you would walk away." Jett grabs my hands, and I let him. "Every day I spent with you, the more I fell."

"You should've told me. I would've gone along with it. Instead, you made me believe you had real feelings for me." I am starting to cry again.

"But I do have feelings for you. I didn't plan on it, and I didn't go looking for it. You are an amazingly kind, beautiful, and fucking sexy woman. If you give me a chance, I'll prove to you that you and I deserve to see if we belong together."

I can see the sincerity on his face, but can I trust this isn't an act? "You made me a laughingstock. I've had people calling me, wanting interviews. There have been photographers taking my picture, to what? Make fun of me."

Jett pulls out his phone and taps away on it. He hands it to me. "That's going to be in *People* magazine tomorrow."

It's a picture of him and then there are pictures of us. The headline reads. *"Jett Hamilton gets real: Hollywood bad boy gone good."* I read the article and it is basically the story of us. He takes responsibility for everything that happened. My eyes burn when I read the last line. *"If she lets me, I'll make it up to her no matter how long it takes."*

"It'll be online too." He takes his phone and stuffs it in his back pocket. "I'm going to go, but here." Jett hands me a little envelope. "That's the key to the suite and the address to where I am staying. My flight leaves tomorrow, but I hope to see you tonight. I'll have dinner waiting at seven."

Pulling me into his arms, he kisses me deeply and turns before walking back to the SUV waiting for him.

I place my fingers against my lips. They still tingle, and I'm in a fog. Suddenly I'm surrounded by my sisters, except for Heidi They're firing off questions, and my eyes flit to each of them.

"What did he say?" That was Mona.

"He is so much hotter in person." That was Sierra.

"What happened?" Miles asks as he wraps his arm around Victoria's waist. "Do I need to go after him and kick his ass?"

"No." Tears begin to slide down my cheeks. "God, I've missed him." I shake my head. "I shouldn't go, right? I mean, what he did humiliated me. I shouldn't care, right?"

"We can't tell you that, honey." Mona wraps her arm around my waist. "What happened?"

I take a deep breath. "He apologized, and he told me he fired his manager. Umm... he showed me an article that's going to come out tomorrow. It is about us and him wanting to make things right." I hold up his room key. "He gave me this, and he wants me to come to his hotel tonight."

"Are you going to go?" Sierra asks while gently bouncing a sleeping Ember.

Shaking my head, I shrug. "I don't know. What if he hurts me again?"

Miles kisses my cheek. "I'll leave you ladies to chat." He heads inside with the others.

Mona moves to stand in front of me. "You can't guarantee that he won't. Hell, you could easily hurt him." She signals to the others. "We wouldn't be where we are now, and Heidi wouldn't be with Colton if we let fear rule us."

"I like the way he looked at you and the way he kissed you." Sierra fans her face. "Phew, it was hot. But seriously, I could've lost Nick if I didn't let go of my fear."

"But what if we don't work out?"

Victoria smiles. "What if you do? What if he's the best thing that's ever happened to you? He flew all the way here to see you. What does that say?"

I nod. "You're right. I've got to go."

I kiss my sisters and Victoria goodbye. I climb into my car and head home to get ready, for what I'm not sure.

# twenty three

## JETT

I check the time and see that Greta should've been here ten minutes ago if she was coming. Fuck, maybe I did blow this. I shouldn't have waited this long. I should've come right away. I lean in, blowing out the candles.

A beep sounds, and then I hear the door open slowly. My heart races as I move toward the hallway. There she is in a pair of black leggings, ballet flats, and a lavender long-sleeve T-shirt. She freezes when she sees me.

Fuck she's beautiful. "I've missed you," I say and then she's running at me.

Greta jumps into my arms, and her lips are on mine. Suddenly it's like everything is as it should be. We move blindly through the suite into the bedroom.

I toss her onto the bed and follow her down. She pushes on me until I fall to my back. My gaze travels up and down her body. She cages me in with her arms and bends down until our lips touch in a slow glide.

Greta controls the kiss, or at least I let her for now. She grinds against me and moans into my mouth. I roll us again and nestle between her legs.

"Beautiful" I whisper as I brush her hair out of her face.

"I missed you too, you know."

We begin ripping each other's clothes off. I begin kissing down her body. Stopping to tug on each nipple ring with my teeth and then sucking her nipples into my mouth. I moan at the feel of them against my tongue.

Working my way down between her thighs, my cock gets rock hard when I see the way her pussy glistens. At the first swipe of her tongue, I moan as her spicy, sweet flavor explodes on my tongue. I groan and feel her reach down, gripping my head. I begin eating her pussy like a man starving for his last meal. I suck her clit into my mouth and ease one finger inside her and then begin to work in another.

I begin tapping that ridged spot inside her that no one else has ever found. The wet sounds of her body is music to my ears. I increase the pressure and suck harder. In no time, she's soaring.

Easing her down, I slowly made my way back up her body. I reach her mouth, and she moans as she tastes herself on my lips. Grabbing her legs, I wrap them around my hips. A moan slips past my lips as I line up my cock with her entrance. I begin easing inside her and groan once I'm fully seated inside her.

"Fuck, being inside of you is better than anything I've experienced," I groan as I begin to fuck her with slow deep strokes.

Our eyes lock as I feel her flutter around me. She reaches in between us and rubs her clit until the desire to come overtakes me. Greta grabs my face, pulling it down to kiss me as she begins to come. I swallow her cries and begin to fuck her harder.

The tingle begins at the base of my spine, and I begin to thrust erratically into her as I begin to come. I swear my eyes are going to roll into the back of my head, but I don't stop. Bathing her channel with my cum, over and over. My never-ending orgasm finally stops. I pant against Greta's neck as she wraps her limbs around me. Nuzzling behind her ear, I take in her sweet scent.

"Am I smashing you?"

"No. Sorry I was late. Traffic was moving so slow." She kisses my forehead and sighs. "I'm glad you came."

"I'm glad I came too." Reluctantly, I pull my softening cock from her. I situate us so I'm on my back and she's snuggled into my side with her arm around my waist. Burying my nose in her hair, I inhale the scent of strawberries. "Are you hungry?"

Her stomach growls, making me laugh. "I'll take that as a yes. Come on, baby." I climb out of bed and grab her ankle.

Greta yelps as I pull her out. I set her on her feet and grab my shirt off the floor.

She smiles as she lifts her arms up and I slip my shirt on her. While she pulls her hair out of the shirt and the blue fabric hits her midthigh. I grab my boxer briefs, slip them on, and then grab her hand.

In the little dining area, she walks around the table, stopping to sniff the flowers I ordered for her. Our food is under silver domes. I pull out her chair for her.

"I wasn't sure what you would want to eat, so I got steaks."

She starts clapping excitedly. "These look great and I'm so hungry. Apparently, my appetite has returned." Her cheeks immediately turn red and she looks down. "Sorry."

I come around and squat down next to her, grabbing her chin to make me look at her. "No, don't be sorry. I'm sorry, Greta. I'm sorry I hurt you, that I embarrassed you, and that I wasn't honest with you."

"How do we make this work?" She rubs her fingers through my hair. "Long distance relationships don't usually work."

I have thought a lot about this and how we could make this work. "That is the best part. We can do whatever we want—whatever works for us. All I know is that I want to try because I'm falling in love with you, Greta Collins."

# GRETA

I swallow Jett's cum as I crawl up his body and lie down on top of him.

He wraps his arms around me, giving me a squeeze. "Fuck, I love your mouth." He pulls me up so he can kiss my mouth, not even caring that his cum was just in it.

Jett puts his hands behind his head, and I rest my chin on mine. He doesn't speak and neither do I, instead we just smile at each other, like a couple of dorks. I yawn a bit later and rest my head on his chest, sighing.

"You make a good mattress." I kiss him right over his heart. "I'm sleepy."

He flips us and with some quick maneuvering, my back is snug against his front and Jett's arm is around my waist. After kissing the back of my head, we snuggle in, and it's not long until he starts snoring softly.

I'm not sure where this is going to go, but that man has pierced my heart and I can't wait to see where life takes us.

# epilogue

## GRETA
### *one year later*

"Are you excited?" Mona asks from the laptop.

I wanted them to see my dress I'm wearing to the premiere of Jett's movie, *Vague Shadows*. I'm so excited but scared to death. I just don't want to embarrass him. This is his night, and I want him to shine. A lot has happened this past year.

It's been babies galore in our family. Heidi and Colton had little Cole, who is my little buddy. Sierra and Nick already have Ember, but they just added another little girl to their brood. Little miss Esme is her big sister's twin. Mona and Joaquin are married now, and she's due any day now with their first baby together, a little boy we can't wait to meet.

Victoria and Miles just got married, and she's pregnant with their first baby too. See, babies everywhere. I love it because I spoil them all every chance I get. I want kids, but I'm not ready yet. Jett and I want to travel and just be together for now. Kids have come up in our conversations, but we just aren't ready yet.

Jett did get the role of Grayson and they shot the movie just outside of Atlanta. Instead of staying at a hotel or renting a home, Jett stayed with me. Of course, I didn't see him a whole lot while he was shooting, but I understood that was his job.

I helped him read lines, which was a lot of fun. He is so good at what he does and getting to watch Jett get into character was fascinating. Getting to come to the set was awesome. Most everyone was super nice, and I got to watch them film a couple of scenes.

His parents flew into Atlanta to visit, and I got to meet them. His mom, Taryn, and his father, Gregory, were so sweet and got along great with my family. My parents even came to town to meet them all. It was mass chaos, but I'd never been happier.

Three months ago, Jett sold his house in California, and bought a four-bedroom, five-bathroom cape cod-style home here in Atlanta. I moved in with him and when I offered to help pay, it didn't go well. After a pretty bad fight, he sat me down.

"Baby, let me do this. I can afford it and I want a beautiful home for us to come home to every time we leave town." He then kissed me, and I had forgotten what I was pissed about.

The studio is doing great and we're busier than ever. Lainey is doing amazing and has started doing larger pieces. We have taken on another apprentice and Gia is a welcome addition. Security has become a constant staple due to all our very overprotective men.

Best of all, I'm in love. It's only been a year, but I truly believe he's it for me. He feels the same way, and he certainly likes to show it.

"Hello? Earth to Greta?" Mona singsongs.

I shake my head. "Sorry, yeah, I'm super excited but nervous." Stepping back, facing the laptop. I hold out my arms. "How do I look?"

My dress is black and shimmery. It's form-fitting, showing off my figure. The sleeves are long, and the back is open. I had my hair styled in a loose chignon and have black diamond earrings in my ears.

"Holy shit. You look amazing." She claps her hands. "My sister is a babe."

Rolling my eyes, I laugh. "Thank you."

Jett comes in, he's wearing a black suit with a blue dress shirt, no tie. His light brown hair is styled, and he's freshly shaved. He freezes when he sees me.

"Fuck, you're gorgeous." Stalking toward me, he pulls me into his arms and kisses me stupid.

"Phew... that was hot." We turn to the laptop and Mona is smiling at us. "Hi Jett, you look great."

"Thanks, Mona." We say goodbye and then I shut the laptop. "Are you ready to head downstairs?"

Ugh... my palms begin to sweat, but I take his hand and we head downstairs.

We're the last car in the line, and there are people everywhere. Jett's manager, Ted, sits across from us. He's super nice and very professional. "Don't worry about Greta. She'll stick with me unless they want pictures of the two of you."

He's my dad's age and certainly has that fatherly feel to him, but he happens to be very good at his job.

The car stops in front of the red carpet, and I swear I'm going to pass out. Already the cameras are flashing, and people are calling his name. The door opens, and he quickly kisses me before climbing out. People scream his name, and he gives a wave before reaching for my hand and helping me out.

I follow behind him as he walks the red carpet. He's a pro, smiles for the camera, and stops talking to reporters. When it's time for pictures, he pulls me to him several times for pictures. I hope I don't look stupid next to him.

Before tonight, I'd asked him if he wanted me to try and get my ink all covered up and take out my facial piercings, but he told me no. He fell in love with me, tattoos and all.

Once we were inside, I go with Ted to sit and wait for the movie to start. I'm pleasantly surprised when we have front-row seats, and when Jett joins us, he sits right next to me. The director stands up to say a few words. He finishes and smiles at Jett.

"Grayson was made for you, Jett. You embodied everything that he was. I just want you to know that I am so proud to have worked with you, all of you. You guys made this project so easy, and I just wanted to say thank you."

The lights go down, and the movie starts.

It's two hours later, and when the credits roll, everyone stands up, clapping. I stand as I wipe the tears from my eyes. The movie was fabulous, and my man was amazing. If he doesn't get nominated for some sort of award, I'll be shocked.

Of course, I know nothing about how they pick their nominees. By the time we get back to the hotel, we're both exhausted and we barely get our clothes off before we both collapse on the bed. The day after tomorrow, we'll head back to Atlanta.

"Thank you for coming with me," he says quietly. "I love you, baby."

I kiss him deeply. "I love you too."

We're both hit with a second wind, and it's a long time before either of us gets any sleep.

# GRETA
## *five years later*

Rolling over in bed, I find Jett's side of the bed empty, and the sheets are cold. I climb out of bed and stretch my arms above my head. A kick to the ribs pulls my attention to my swollen belly. Rubbing my hands over it, my son gives a little kick.

In the bathroom, I use the facilities, and after I wash my hands, I brush my teeth. Back in our bedroom, I grab a pair of fuzzy socks because my feet always get cold. On top of the dresser is a picture of Jett and me, along with Miles and Victoria, and Bruno and his fiancée, Rose. We were at the Emmy awards.

About three years ago, Jett, Miles, and Bruno turned one of my brother's books into a TV series script. It got picked up by one of the big streaming services. Jett plays Detective Jameson Edwards and Bruno has a small role as his best friend, Sterling.

They wanted Miles to be part of the whole process. He is the head writer, and I've loved seeing them all working together. They just finished shooting season two last month. Since season one was such a huge hit, their budget was even bigger for this one.

They won two Emmys for the show, they won best screenwriting, and my man won best actor. When they called his name, I think I screamed like a crazy person. I watched with tears in my eyes as he accepted the award. He was humble and grateful and has definitely changed people's opinion of him over the years.

It happened when *Vague Shadows* released. Although he didn't win, he was nominated for an Oscar for best actor.

We got married last year in Key West. It was a small, intimate affair. Our families both flew down for the festivities and then we went back to Greece for our honeymoon.

I step out into the hall and hear soft music playing from the nursery. Padding my way across the hall, I find my gorgeous husband sitting on the floor, putting together the baby's crib.

He smiles when he sees me. "Good morning, beautiful." Jett holds out his hand to me. I take it, and *try* to bend down to kiss him, but instead he stands, pulling me into his arms. "Did you sleep well?"

I nod and snuggle close, or as close as I can with my belly. "I did. I thought we were going to have an all-morning snuggle fest." Pouting, I kiss his chin.

"We were, but I couldn't sleep and thought I'd get to work on the crib. I can't believe he'll be here in a month." Jett is all about the baby and pregnancy. He has gone to every appointment with me. "We need to pick a name."

That has been one of the most difficult things. Every name I come up with, he shoots down and every name he comes up with I don't like.

"I have been thinking, and what about waiting until he's here and we see what name fits him."

"Whatever you want." He rubs my belly. "Isn't

that right, Harrison?"

"Harrison?" Our son gives a huge kick. "I think he likes it. We'll keep it on the back burner for sure."

I smile up at him and shake my head. "I love you, Mr. Hamilton."

"Well, I love you, Mrs. Hamilton."

My man leads me into the kitchen, and he makes me breakfast.

Going on our adventure was the best decision I ever made, and three weeks later, our little man, Harrison Jett Hamilton, joined our family, and we're both so in love.

# author's NOTE

Thank you so much for reading my Sugar and Spice Ink series!! God, I've loved writing their stories. I honestly don't think I could pick a favorite because I love them all. Keep an eye out because the kids will get their own stories.

Again, thank you so much for loving the Collins family!

*Evan*

# meet
# EVAN

A Midwesterner and a readaholic most of her life until one day an idea came into Evan's head and a writing career was born. She's a sucker for happily ever afters and loves creating fictional worlds that others can get lost in. She loves putting her characters through the ringer, but loves when they get to that satisfying, swoony ending.

When the voices in her head give it a rest, which isn't often, she can always be found with her e-reader in her hand. Some of her favorites include, Aurora Rose Reynolds, (the queen) Kristen Ashley, Kaylee Ryan, Natasha Madison, and Harper Sloan. Evan finds a lot of her inspiration in music, movies, TV shows and life.

She's a wife to Jim and a mom to Ethan and (the real)Evan, a weightlifter, a home healthcare scheduler, and a full-time author. How does she do it? She'll never tell.

# acknowledgments

First and foremost, thank you to my husband Jim. Whenever I'm on a deadline, you always step in, handling the cooking and cleaning while I work. I don't know how I'll ever be able to repay you, but I'm sure I'll think of something.

To my amazing ARC team, thank you from the bottom of my heart for your never ending support. I know sometimes I like to spring those new releases on you, but you still give me your all.

Evan's Entourage, my most excellent readers group. Thank you from the bottom of my heart for your support and enthusiasm, I love you all.

To Ellie thank you for helping make my story the best it could be. I know I was so late and set you up last minute, but you always find a way to help. I appreciate you!!

Ben my amazing cover designer, thank you for making me the most perfect and most beautiful cover ever. It was like you crawled in my head and knew exactly what I wanted. This may be my favorite one.

Ashley, oh my god! Thank you for helping me with TikTok. It's been a career changer and it's all thanks to you!! <3

Also, a quick thank you to anyone who has ever read any of my books, thank you for letting me live my dream.

check out these
other titles from
EVAN GRACE

*"A single parent, opposites attract romance that will captivate you from the very first page"*
**- New York Times bestselling author, Kaylee Ryan**

Ordinary, typical, conformed, are words never used to describe me. I've never been one to play by the rules. It's my world, my life and I do things my way.

I see the way they stare at my body covered in tattoos and my lavender hair, I just don't give a damn. There is only one thing in this world that can get me fired up, that's screwing with my daughter. As a single mom, it's my job to protect her, fight for her. She is and will always be my top priority.

So, when I get a call that she's in trouble at school, with a boy- no less, my claws are out and ready to strike. And the boy's father, some high society stockbroker, isn't about to deter me. I don't care how sexy, smart and rugged he is.

Opposites may attract, and I've been down that road before, it's one I never plan to travel again. A man like that would never be interested in a woman like me. That I know for certain, after all I'm a realist.

# *one*

## MONA

My alarm clock blares, causing me to groan. Those last couple tequila shots last night were such a mistake. Tequila has never been my friend, and I don't know why I thought last night would be any different. I push myself up into a sitting position, but that is a mistake because it feels like my brain is rattling around in my skull. I grab my head as I crawl out of bed and gingerly make my way into the bathroom.

After quickly relieving myself, I grab a bottle of Ibuprofen out of the medicine cabinet. I shake a couple into my hand, pop them into my mouth, and stick my mouth under the faucet. After swallowing them down, I shuffle back to my bed, crawl under the covers, and pray for death.

While buried under my blankets I feel my orange tabby,

Peanut, jump on the bed, spin in circles, and then snuggle into my side. As soon as his furry ass begins to purr, I feel my eyes get heavy and let sleep pull me under.

I finally feel semi-human and climb out of bed, heading back into the bathroom. I brush my lavender-colored locks up into a bun on top of my head and jump into the shower. Once I'm scrubbed clean I feel more like myself.

Back in the bedroom, I throw on a pair of black leggings, white camisole, and a blue off-the-shoulder t-shirt. I pad through the house and stick a piece of bread in the toaster and brew some coffee. When the toast is done, I slather it in Nutella and then pour myself a cup of coffee.

Keys jingle, and the front door flies open. My reason for living comes running into the kitchen. "Mommy!"

I catch my daughter and lift her into my arms. "How's my beautiful girl? Were you good for Uncle Miles?"

My brother leans against the open doorway. "She was perfect as always. We had a blast, didn't we, Goober?"

"Yep, Uncle Miles bought me lots and lots of candy."

Of course, he did. My brother has been such an incredible help with Iris, but the man can't ever tell my daughter no. I set her on the ground. "Why don't you go put your dirty clothes in the hamper, and go play with Peanut because I know he missed you."

She kisses me and my brother before running out of the kitchen, yelling for our cat. I grab my brother a cup of coffee, and we sit at the little dinette in front of the window. "How was your girls' night?"

"It was good. Sierra was in rare form and forced me to do two shots of tequila after mass quantities of beer, and then I had to Uber it home."

There are four daughters and one son in our crazy family. I'm the oldest, then Sierra, Miles is in between us four girls, and then there are Greta and Heidi. We're super close, especially Miles and me. Maybe because he stepped in to be there when Iris' dad split, which was basically the moment the pregnancy test came back positive.

"I'm sure she had to twist your arm too." He stands and pulls me up into a hug. "I'm gonna take off. I've got a book to plot." Miles is a crime fiction writer and, the amazing man he is, a New York Times Bestselling author.

"Have fun with that, and thanks again for keeping Iris." I smile up at him.

"You know I'd do anything for my girls." He calls out goodbye to my daughter, and she comes running out to her uncle.

Iris launches herself into his arms. "Bye, Uncle Miles."

"I'll pick you up tomorrow from Kiddie college."

He leaves, and I smile down at my champagne blonde-haired, blue-eyed angel. "Today is a Mommy/Daughter day. We're going to make a veggie pizza, some chocolate chip cookies, and have couch snuggles."

"Yay! Can you polish my nails?"

I nod. "Of course."

She hops up and down. Her joy is infectious, and we start our Mommy/Daughter day, which indeed ends with snuggles on the couch.

At the end of our day, I tuck her into bed, brushing her hair out of her face. Iris gives me that smile that's like a balm to my soul. "Sleep well, baby girl."

"I love you," she whispers before rolling to her side and closes her eyes. I don't move right away; I sit and watch as she falls asleep. The steady rise and fall of her chest signals she's out.

From the moment she was born I've watched her sleep more times than I can count. She's the best thing I've ever done, and Iris makes me proud every day.

Is everything always rainbows and unicorns? No, definitely not, but my girl can handle anything thrown our way.

"What do you mean they want to have a meeting about Iris?" I look down at the paper that my brother brought to me after he picked up Iris from Kiddie College. He dropped her off at the tattoo studio I own with my sisters, just like he does every day.

Sierra and I started Sugar and Spice, Ink four years ago. We're all artistic and fell in love with tattoos and piercings. When I decided that I wanted to be a tattoo artist, I met with the one who did a lot of the ink on my body and got him to agree to mentor me. As his apprentice, I cleaned up the shop and answered phones all while learning to tattoo.

Sierra followed in my footsteps almost a year later.

Over the past four years, we've worked our asses off to make a name for ourselves. Because our studio is exclusively female artists, a lot of people didn't take us seriously. We had to work hard to get word of mouth referrals and prove we were just as talented.

We started getting followers on social media and really used the power of the web to make a name for ourselves. Now, four years later, we've been featured in Ink'd magazine twice, we've been interviewed on Atlanta's morning news, and we were even approached for a reality show, but declined.

I focus back on Miles. "I'm not sure, but they want you there tomorrow morning."

Miles and I step out of my office and head into the main part of the studio. I'm always in awe of the place we've created. The walls are a deep purple, almost an eggplant color, with white swirls. Our tables and chairs are black and chrome.

We have a lot of our artwork on the walls in frames. Some of the tattoos on display are ours, and Greta is on display for her piercings. My favorite photo is of the four of us girls in black Sugar and Spice Ink, sleeveless t-shirts, jean shorts, and red Converse. Heidi did our hair and makeup pin-up girl style.

We find my daughter and Sierra sitting in the waiting area drawing together. Through the entrance to the back, I hear the buzz of a tattoo machine, which is so fucking relaxing.

"Hey, sweet girl, why do they want me to come into the school and talk to them?"

She doesn't look up from her drawing. "I kissed Max," Iris says it so matter-of-factly that I'm taken aback.

"Who's Max?"

"Max Pena. He's my best friend." She has a smile on her lips. Man, I'm in trouble with this girl.

I sit next to her. "Did he not want you to kiss him, is that why I have to go in?"

She shakes her head. "No, he wanted me to," Iris says.

I don't have much longer to think about that because my last appointment of the day has just shown up. Since I have Iris, my sisters and I agreed it best if I open the shop daily, then I can get out of there by five or six, and I love them for it.

After my appointment, I clean up my workstation and find my girl in my office watching Tangled on my iPad. "Are you ready to head home, baby girl?"

"Yep."

I help her gather her stuff, and then hand in hand we head out to the work area and say our goodbyes.

Once we get home I make us some veggie quesadillas. Iris and I are vegetarians, which I wasn't until I was up in the middle of the night with a newborn and watched a documentary about where our meat comes from. After that, I just couldn't do it. I didn't set out to make Iris one too, but she loves to do what her mom does.

We eat at our little table in the kitchen, and she tells me about her day at Kiddie College. Things have been much easier this summer with Iris able to go there during the day.

After dinner, we snuggle on the couch and watch Modern Family. I can tell she's getting tired when she starts slowly tracing the tattoo of her name on my forearm. Sierra did it for me when Iris was a year old. *Iris* is done in beautiful calligraphy surrounded by gorgeous flowers.

Before she falls asleep, I maneuver her to the bathroom so she can go and then brush her teeth. In her bedroom, she changes into her pink nightgown with sugar skulls all over it.

Iris climbs onto her bed and under her purple butterfly-covered comforter. "Are you all snuggled in?"

"Yes, Mommy." I know my girl's tired. She only calls me Mommy when she's sleepy—much to my chagrin. "Will you lay with me?"

I crawl into bed with her and lean against the headboard. She rests her little blonde head in my lap. "Do you want me to tell you a story?"

She yawns and nods. "Tell me about the day I was born."

Iris has always preferred my stories over the ones in storybooks. I stroke my hand over her soft wavy locks. This is her favorite story, even though it was the easiest labor and delivery ever. "Okay, baby girl. It was two days before your due date, and I was working at a little tattoo studio by Georgia State." My mind goes back to that day...

My back aches, but I ignore it while I continue working on this arm piece. I've worked on this piece for four hours this go around and four hours a month ago. That time was just the outline and details. Today I'm doing the coloring.

I don't know why I keep working. My due date is fast approaching, and it's been so hard to work with my big, protruding belly, but I wanted to keep going as long as possible and to make as much money before his or her arrival.

I never expected to become a mother at twenty-two, especially a single one—no one does—but I'm ready and prepared. I'm just wiping off my client's tattoo. I let her stand and take a look at it in the mirror, smiling as she squeals with delight.

She comes back over, and I wipe some ointment on it before putting plastic wrap over it. I stand to walk her to the counter when I feel a trickle down my leg. "Oh shit."

Buck, the owner, is sitting behind the desk and looks up at my exclamation. The girl I just finished working on turns toward me as well. "Did you just pee your pants?" She laughs.

"No! Of course not, my water just broke." I turn to Buck. "Can you take care of her? I'm calling Sierra."

"You've got it, doll. Good luck."

By the time my sister comes to bring me to the hospital, my contractions are four minutes apart. On the way, I called my mom, and she's meeting us there.

Two hours later, I'm now dressed in only a sports bra and squatting in the water while leaning against the side of the pool, moaning through my contractions. I wanted a natural childbirth, and my midwife had told me about water birth, so that's what I decided I wanted to do.

My mom and Sierra help me through labor as my contractions grow stronger and extremely close together. As my stomach tightens, I rest my head on the side of the pool, moaning softly as my sister fans me, and my mom places a cool washcloth on my neck.

It isn't long before I'm hit with the desire to push. The midwife checks me and says it's time to start pushing. They have me squat in the water, and I begin to push. After pushing for a half hour, they have me reach down to feel the top of my baby's head. I moan as I push with all of my might, and then I feel the baby slip from my body.

They help me grab the baby, and as soon as they lift her out of the water, my beautiful baby starts to cry. The nurse lifts one of the legs and announces, "It's a girl." I begin to cry and hug my daughter to my chest.

Before my mom even cuts the cord, my daughter is latched onto my breast, nursing happily. I'd go through the pain of losing her dad and the pain of her birth to do it all over again.

"What are you going to name her?" Sierra whispers before kissing my cheek.

I've had a couple names picked out for both boys and girls and kept them to myself. I didn't want anyone to influence my decision. I stare at my beautiful baby girl and whisper, "Iris Clementine Collins."

Clementine was my mom's favorite aunt's name, and Iris because I've always loved it for a little girl's name, and it's my favorite flower. Both Aunt and Grandma lean in whispering their "hellos" to my beautiful baby girl.

"Mommy?"

I look down at Iris. "Yes, baby?"

"I love you." It warms my heart every time she tells me that. I can't imagine my life without her in it.

"Love you too." In seconds she's out, hugging her stuffed unicorn to her chest.

I slip out of her bed, turn on her nightlight, and shut the door. Out in the living room, I light my candles, turn out the lights, and grab my meditation pillow. I set everything up in front of the coffee table and ask my *Alexa* to turn on my *Chill Zone* mix.

On my pillow, I get into full lotus position, close my eyes, and clear my mind. I'm not sure how long I've meditated until I open my eyes and see that a half hour has passed. Peanut is sitting in front of me wearing the same bored expression he always does.

"What?"

He tips his head to the side and gives me a "meow". I reach out and scratch behind his ear and then yawn. His fluffy butt follows me as I lock the front door, check on Iris, and he follows me into the bathroom, watching me as I take care of business in here.

I strip down to my tank top and panties, curling up under the sheets and blanket. Peanut jumps on the bed, and I feel him circle his spot behind my knees before he settles in and begins to purr. Not long after, sleep pulls me under.

# two

## JOAQUIN

I pull my Range Rover into the parking lot of Edgewood Community College where I've been summoned by Mr. G, the head of the kiddie college that my son Max attends. My son's a good kid, so I'm not sure why Mr. G wants to see me, and my son has said zilch.

I turn to my boy in the backseat. "You ready to go inside, *mijo*?"

My mini-me looks up from his tablet and smiles. "Yeah, Dad." He shuts it off and sets it on the seat. I hop out and meet him at the front. Max may be seven, but he's an old soul. I'm blessed to be his dad.

I'm a single father and have been since he was a toddler. His mother and I were never right for each other. She was the daughter of one of my father's associates. She was a gold-digging whore, and I wasn't going to let her lead me around by my dick.

She trapped me by getting pregnant on purpose, but she's definitely not mother material. Melina hired a nanny when Max was barely a week old. I, of course, fired the woman because I grew up with nannies, and that wasn't going to be the way my son grew up.

Max only sees her once or maybe twice a year, and it's usually awkward and confuses my boy. His mom's remarried now and someone else's problem—thank God. My cell phone rings as we walk through the halls toward the office of Mr. G. I look and see that it's my secretary, Lauren. "Hold up, Max. I have to take this." I swipe the screen. "Hey, Lauren."

"Sorry to bother you, Mr. Pena." I roll my eyes because I'm constantly telling her to call me Joaquin, but she refuses. "Your three o'clock appointment called and said that they could reschedule for four-thirty. Correct?"

"Yes, as long as they're my last appointment. I promised Max I'd grill burgers tonight, and I don't want to be at the office late." Max smiles up at me, and I ruffle his brown, shaggy hair. I'll need to make him an appointment for a haircut.

"You're all finished after that. I'll make the arrangements. Shall I have coffee waiting?" Lauren is by far the best secretary I've ever had.

"That would be great, thank you." I disconnect and shove my phone inside the pocket of my favorite dove gray Tom Ford two-piece suit. My shirt is a dark salmon pink color, as is the pocket square, and I'm not wearing a tie. On my feet are my favorite Ferragamo Benson burnished leather loafers.

We turn the corner, and I notice a woman with lavender hair braided and hanging over one shoulder. She looks up as we approach, and I'm hit by some unknown force right in the solar plexus. Her eyes are a sparkling cornflower blue. She's got lips made for kissing—*made for kissing?*

Her sun-kissed arms are covered in gorgeous, colorful tattoos. Her white t-shirt hangs off one dainty shoulder, black legging capris cover her legs, and hot pink Converses cover her feet.

"Iris!" Max runs past me to the beautiful little blonde who looks like her mom's twin, but without the lavender hair and ink.

"Max!" She jumps up, and they hug each other. They move to the opposite bench, talking quietly to each other.

"Um... hi. I'm Mona." The lavender-haired beauty holds out her hand. I take her hand, ignoring how soft and small it feels in my much larger one.

"Mr. Pena and Ms. Collins, I'm Mr. G." I turn away from Mona and look at the short man with a major paunch and thinning hairline.

I don't miss the way he looks at Mona, what with the tattoos and the lavender colored hair; she doesn't look like a lot of the parents who bring their kids here. I hold my hand out, squeezing his hand a little harder than necessary. "I'm Joaquin, Max's dad."

"Pleasure," he says and then holds his hand out to Mona. "Please follow me into my office."

We both sit in front of his desk while the kids are led to one of the classrooms to give us some privacy. Mr. G sits behind his desk like he's all high and mighty.

The man looks between the two of us. "Before we begin, will Mrs. Pena be joining us?"

Had the moron read Max's information he'd see that she's not. "His mother is on vacation with her husband. He lives with me full-time."

The idiot nods. "Yesterday, there was a situation with your kids. It was snack time, and the children weren't with the class, so one of the aides went looking for them. She found the two of them by the bathroom, and they were kissing on the mouth." He crosses his arms and looks between us.

Before I can respond, Mona chimes in, "And???"

"Ms. Collins, we don't tolerate that sort of behavior here." The fat prick scowls at her.

Mona leans forward. "I understand that, but did either of them appear to be in distress?"

"Well no, but they're seven years old, and they shouldn't even know about that stuff." Mr. G stares at Mona with a judgmental look on his face.

Out of the corner of my eye, I see Mona tense, gripping the armrests of her chair. She looks ready to snap, and I do the only thing I can think of and put my hand on her knee. I don't miss the way she freezes, and I certainly don't miss the way she trembles under my hand.

I remove it and ignore the fact that it made my dick twitch and my pulse race a little. I open my mouth to speak, but Mona chimes in again. "They shouldn't know about that stuff? I beg your pardon, but people kiss in cartoons. My daughter sees her grandparents kiss. I'm not going to make her feel ashamed that she did it." She stands. "I will talk to her about sneaking off with her friends, and she won't do that again."

"Ms. Collins, I can see you're upset, but the kids aren't in trouble. We just wanted to make you aware of what happened, and maybe you both could discuss with them what is and isn't proper behavior in school." He stands from behind his desk. "I want you to know that your daughter is a joy to have in our creative writing class. She's got a natural gift."

We follow him into the classroom that's off his office and find Iris and Max sitting together coloring. Mona sits across from them. "That's a great tree, Max."

My boy smiles up at her. "Your hair is pretty." He's a charmer, that's for sure.

Mona reaches across the table and grabs Max's arm. "Thank you. Iris, come give me a hug goodbye. Uncle Miles will pick you up and bring you to the studio, okay."

"Yes, Mom. I love you."

I walk around the table, ruffling Max's hair. "I'll be back after my meeting to get you. I love you, *mijo*."

As soon as I leave the classroom I spot Mona up ahead, but I don't rush to catch up with her; there's no point. Like I said, she's not my type. Plus, my focus needs to be on my son, not pussy.

I head downtown to my office. I have to prep before my meeting. My partners and I keep things flexible, which is great and I'm able to get off at a reasonable time so I can still be a father to my boy. My father is a workaholic, and growing up I watched as my mom grew to resent him.

They both began screwing around on each other, and that led to a nasty divorce. Now they live on opposite sides of the country. Dad is on marriage number four, and Mom is on marriage number two, but things are rocky.

When I divorced Max's mom I swore, I was never going to get married again. She reminded me exactly why I wanted to always stay single, but I'll never regret my boy. Once I reach the office, I park in the garage and head to the elevator, taking it up to my floor.

I share a floor with a marketing agency, but they're on one side, and I'm on the other. My partners and I have had our own brokerage firm for the past three years. Before that, I worked for my father's firm. When he decided to retire down in Florida, his partners became mine, and his clients followed me.

Our receptionist for the office greets me from his desk. "Good morning, Shane."

"Morning. I love that suit; it's my favorite," he says with his usual flourish. The man basically runs the office and is my personal shopper. He and Lauren are the backbone of the company. I'd be lost without either of them. He flirts with me a little, but it doesn't bother me; he's harmless.

I shake my head and head toward the back. Lauren stands as I approach. "How was the meeting?"

"My son and a little girl snuck off, and when they found them they were kissing on the lips. Iris is his best friend I guess. Anyway, the guy was a pompous ass. Iris' mom let him have it."

"My boys were rascals like that when they were his age. I'm sure it was harmless." Her boys are in their early twenties, and even though I'm thirty she treats me like one of her kids, but not in an obnoxious way. "I've got the conference room set up for your meeting. When they arrive, shall I bring you coffee?" She follows me into my office.

"That would be great." Lauren hands me my messages and then closes the door behind her, letting me get to work.

I pull into the winding driveway that leads to the modern cottage I bought two years ago in the Buckhead district when I decided Max and our damn dog, Fluffy, needed more room to play.

When we moved here, my cousin Victoria moved in with us. Her mom is my dad's sister, and she's about as maternal as my dad is paternal. Thank God we have each other. She's been a big help with my son.

Her moving in with me was only supposed to be temporary, but with as much as she does for us, we decided we'd keep our arrangement until she either needed to move on or I met someone.

Victoria was given the task of decorating. I only had two stipulations: nothing girly and nothing bachelor pad-ish. Don't get me wrong, I have expensive taste, but I wanted a home that my son could feel like he could play in.

I grew up in a home where I was told not to make a mess and to never run around and be a kid. I pull into the garage and hop out with my boy following me. As soon as we step inside, the scent of tomatoes hits me. Victoria is a maestro in the kitchen.

"*Tia* Victoria, we're home." Max runs through the mudroom and into the kitchen where I find him hugging my cousin.

"How was school? What did they want to talk to you about?" She asks me the second part.

"Max and a girl named Iris were caught kissing," I say.

"Oh, I love Iris. Why did you kiss her?" She squats in front of Max.

The little shit rolls his eyes. "She's my best friend." The way he says it he should've ended with a *duh*. Max crosses his arms. "They wouldn't let us sit together."

I'm not a hundred percent sure how to handle this because I don't want him to feel shame. "If she's your best friend, why did you kiss her?"

"You kiss *Tia* Victoria, and she's your best friend." Well, he has me there.

"That's true, buddy, she is, and yes, I kiss her, but only on the cheek or forehead—not the lips, definitely not the lips. Got it?"

He nods. "I've got it. Do you think she could come over and play sometime?"

Iris' mom, with her lavender hair, pops into my head. They're both beautiful, and I imagine Mona's natural hair is the same as her daughter's. She definitely had some gumption, not letting that fat fuck shame her. I push thoughts of her away—not going there.

"Yeah, maybe we could have her over one afternoon." I walk over and look at what Victoria has cooking. "I was going to grill burgers."

"Go ahead, this sauce is for dinner tomorrow night. I just wanted to get it done so we didn't have to worry about it tomorrow. I've got the patties already made and in the fridge." She looks down at my son. "You can help me make homemade fries."

I head to the master bedroom, which is on the first floor, and change into a pair of jeans and a t-shirt. Fluffy comes tearing into my room; he must've been outside when we got home. He reads me his puppy riot act for being gone. I pick his white curly-haired ass up and hug him to my chest while he licks my neck.

He's a Shih Tzu/Poodle mix and is the best dog we could ask for. "Are you a good boy?" Fluffy pants in my face. "Your breath is horrid." I scratch behind his ear and then set him down.

*He follows me to the two people I love more than anything.*

**Free on Kindle Unlimited**

# AFTER WE MET

Gorgeous. Sweet. Funny. He made me feel things that I've never felt before. In just one short week over Spring Break, I began to fall in love. That is until it all fell apart. Now, here I am, three years later and I've moved on, at least that's what I told myself until he came crashing back into my life. Things have changed. I've changed, and there's something he doesn't know.

He wants me to give us another chance. I try to fight it, but it's not long before all of those same old feelings come rushing back. I know he feels it too. I can see it every time he looks at me. I can feel it every time he touches me.

It feels like I'm missing something though, like there's something that he's not telling me. Something that has the potential to tear it all apart. After all, it's not easy when you fall in love with your best friends' father. I didn't stand a chance after we met.

# CHAPTER ONE
### *Lani*

"Are you sure your dad is okay with me tagging along? I don't want to get in the way of your visit." My best friend, Molly, sits down next to my carry-on bag as I stuff my toiletries inside it.

She grabs my hand before I can zip the bag shut. "Of course he doesn't care. He said it'd be good if I brought someone just because he may have to run to the bar. Plus, he says that he's pretty boring and I'd want someone to go dancing with."

Molly's dad paid for my plane ticket, and when I refused to accept it, she made sure to let me know that her dad got non-refundable tickets. Molly told her dad that I'd refuse them—that's why he did it.

Of course he was taking a gamble that something would keep one or both of us from going.

"Okay, I am pretty excited to swim in the ocean."

I've never really been anywhere, and I've certainly never been to the coast. Growing up, it was just my mom and me. I never knew my dad, and my mom sometimes had to work two or three jobs to keep food on the table and clothes on my back.

I met Molly our freshman year at the U of I in Iowa City. We're both elementary education students.

Now we're on spring break of our senior year. She and I are both so ready to be done and get teaching jobs. Part of the reason she wants me to go with her to Florida is that once we're both out in the real world, one or both of us could end up moving away.

My mom and I have had the discussion multiple times. We're super close, but she also knows that I'll need to go where the work is.

"Hello?" Molly waves her hand in front of my face. "Where'd you go?"

I shake my head. "Nowhere, just spaced out for a second. Are we taking an Uber to the airport?"

"Yeah, I figure that way we don't have to worry about parking." She reaches out, grabbing one of my sable locks. "Your hair grows so fast. I'm so jealous of your curls." She's one to talk. My gorgeous friend has sleek sheets of auburn hair, sparkling blue eyes, and a willowy body—with great breasts.

Me, on the other hand, I've got dark hair and eyes, light tan skin and I'm pretty muscular. I joined Crossfit after I gained my freshman thirty. Now I've got muscles and I'm fucking strong. Molly assures me all of the time that my body is still girly.

I grab my bag and Molly stands up. We're dressed almost exactly the same. We're both in black leggings, long sleeve t-shirts with zipped up hoodies over them. I'm wearing a beat-up old pair of Adidas and she's wearing Nikes.

She orders our Uber as I carry my bag and tote out into the living room and set them down next to Molly's stuff. Nervous anticipation fills me because I've never flown before, but I downloaded movies on my iPad to distract me and bought some books that I've downloaded on my Kindle.

When the driver is a couple of minutes away, we lock up and head downstairs.

It takes us about a half hour to get to the airport. After checking in and going through security, we make our way to our gate. We sit next to each other—I pull out my Kindle and she pulls out her phone.

Molly grabs her bottle of Xanax out of her purse and breaks one in half and hands it to me. "This is a low dose. It'll help take the edge off."

I take it, pop it in my mouth, and wash it down with my bottle of water. My knee bounces up and down while we wait to begin boarding. By the time we're getting on the plane, I feel loosey-goosey. I follow Molly to our seats, and I give her the window seat because I don't think I'm ready for that yet.

When we're ready to take off, I ask Molly to tell me more about her dad. I know that he and Molly's mom weren't married for very long, and he owns his own bar down in Key West. They had her young, and unfortunately he moved away due to his job and she didn't get to see him as often as she'd like.

Her dad's supposed to be the complete opposite of her mom. Molly says he's a free spirit and a bit wild, but a good and loving dad. I've seen pictures and he's definitely hot. He looks like Samantha's boyfriend from *Sex and the City.* I'm sure the women hang all over him.

When we finally land, the sun is starting to set. I look out Molly's window and am in awe of the view. The water looks dark blue, and I can't wait to see it in the sunshine. As soon as the seatbelt light goes off, Molly pulls out her phone. "I'm texting Dad that we're here."

I stand up and stretch my poor body—fuck me, there's no room on these planes. Molly grabs our bags out of the overhead compartment and hands me mine. I follow closely behind her as we make our way out of the plane on to the tarmac.

Molly screams, drops her bag, and takes off toward baggage claim. I follow much more sedately and smile as she flings herself at—who I'm assuming is her dad. He sets Molly down and I smile as I watch him hug her tightly.

I hear her say my name, and then they turn toward me. My stomach does a little flip as he smiles at me. Oh God, I can feel my nipples hardening. What if he can tell?

"Lani, come meet my Dad. Dad, this is my bestie, Lani. This crazy man is my dad, Damon." Oh great, even his name is hot.

I reach my hand out. "It's so nice to meet you. Thank you for letting me come with Molly."

He grips my hand in his. I try not to stare at his beautiful face, but I can't help it. His square jaw is covered in light stubble. His blue eyes are highlighted by beautifully long eyelashes, and he's got lines around his eyes that just add to his gorgeousness. He's got that dimple in his chin, and full lips I want to kiss. *What?*

"I'm glad you could come and keep my girl company and you're very welcome." We follow him outside to his black Jeep Wrangler.

The wind blows through my hair as we make our way toward her dad's place. We pull up in front of the cutest little house I've ever seen. It's exactly what you'd expect a house to look like in a beach town. "You girls each have your own room with a Jack and Jill bathroom in between. Your bedrooms are upstairs. Mine is on the main floor."

We step into the house and I'm immediately in love. The floors are a light wood. The walls are a light tan-ish yellow with white trim. The sofa and two chairs are the color of watermelon.

I don't get to look too much before he shows us to our bedrooms upstairs. Full-size mattresses fill both rooms, but Molly's has pictures on the walls and nightstand. A teddy bear also sits on top of her bed. "I'll whip up something for dinner while you get settled."

"Thanks, Dad." Molly hugs him before he disappears downstairs. "Go get your stuff put away and get comfy. We'll rest until dinner is done."

On the way into my room, all I can think is that her dad is hot and it's going to be a long week.

# CHAPTER TWO

### *Damon*

I head downstairs, ignoring the reaction I had to Lani. The moment I laid eyes on her, I felt like I'd been kicked in the gut. I've *never* in my forty-two years *ever* had that reaction to a woman like this before.

Wouldn't it just figure that she's forbidden times two: She's my daughter's best friend and I'm old enough to be her father. I grab the salad out of the refrigerator and the chicken breasts I've had marinating all day. It's a homemade marinade that Molly and I "invented" when she was visiting the summer after her freshman year in high school.

We named it Monroe's special sauce, I know... real original. It's got red wine vinegar, olive oil, soy sauce, garlic, oregano, and it's got a real nice tang to it. I take it out and turn on my gas grill. Once I place the chicken on the grill, I close the lid and run the bowl inside.

I head back outside and take a drink of my beer when arms wrap around my waist. I wrap my arm around Molly's shoulders and hug her into my side, kissing her forehead. This beautiful girl is the best thing I've ever done. I tried making it work with her mom, but she was jealous and never trusted me.

Every time I had to travel and do a shoot, she'd accuse me of cheating, which I never did. It got to be too much, so when Molly was three, we split. At first, I was able to see her a lot, but when the modeling jobs started drying up, I got offered a job and worked for a short time at one of the TV stations here, but I hated it.

I decided to buy an old run-down bar that was no longer open. It took me almost a year to get it to where I wanted it and now *Molly's* is a hot spot. We're right near the water, which makes it a tourist attraction. We're nothing special, no gimmicks, no dance floor, but we still pack them in.

"Oh, is that Monroe's special sauce?" She takes a big whiff and I swear I hear her stomach growl.

"Of course it is. I bought a couple bottles of Riesling for you. I know you said that you liked sweet wines. Tomorrow night I'm throwing you girls a welcoming party. It's nothing big just a few friends that want to see you, and meet Lani."

She gives me another squeeze. "That's great. I've missed you," Molly says quietly. She's always been a daddy's girl even when we were far apart.

"I've missed you too, baby." Out of the corner of my eye, I find Lani standing a few feet away from us looking unsure of herself. "Lani, I hope you like chicken."

She walks toward us. "I do, thanks. Your home is really beautiful, Mr. Monroe."

"Nope, don't call me mister, it makes me feel old." The lights above the grill show off the pink tinge of her cheeks. "Please just call me Damon." I look to my daughter. "Why don't you ladies get a drink and set the table by the pool. Dinner will be ready in about five minutes."

Molly grabs Lani's arm and drags her toward the house. My eyes immediately go to Lani's ass in the little shorts she's wearing. Fuck, her legs go on and on, and... of course she turns and catches me staring at her.

*Free on Kindle Unlimited*

*more titles from*
# EVAN GRACE

www.authorevangrace.com

*stay connected*
# WITH EVAN

**Facebook Author Page** ~ http://bit.ly/2nGpUfQ

**Facebook Reader Group** ~
http://bit.ly/2osdDbR

**Goodreads Author Page** ~
http://bit.ly/2oo7iYH

**Twitter** ~ http://bit.ly/2nGiBon

**Instagram** ~ http://bit.ly/2nusgxW

**Amazon Author Page** ~ http://amzn.to/2nulojT

**Bookbub** ~ www.bookbub.com/profile/evan-grace

**Sign up for my newsletter and get the latest news** ~
http://bit.ly/2ncb8dv

www.ingramcontent.com/pod-product-compliance
Lightning Source LLC
Chambersburg PA
CBHW031041310726
48969CB00007B/2066